G000147776

MY ALIEN

Book One

Robin Martin

Published by Bennett Lane Press 2016
Copyright © 2016 Robin Martin

All rights reserved.

www.robinmartinthomas.com

The characters and events portrayed in this book are fictitious.
Any similarity to real persons, living or dead, is coincidental and
not intended by the author.

No part of this publication may be reproduced, stored in a retrieval
system, or transmitted in any form or by any means, electronic,
mechanical, photocopying, recording or otherwise, without the
prior written permission from the publisher.

A catalogue record for this book is available from the National
Library of Australia.

Book cover design and formatting services by bookcovercafe.com

ISBN:
978-0-9946465-0-7 (pbk)
978-0-9946465-1-4 (e-bk)

For Rosie

*My little writing buddy, who stayed with me
on long summer days and cold winter mornings,
cheering me on with a wag of her tail and always
being ready to share an ANZAC biscuit or two.*

Chapter One

A translucent bubble drifted down from the sky, gently breaking on my forehead.

This is your lucky day. A high-pitched voice sounded in my ears.

I stopped walking and looked around the broad expanse of beach, expecting to see someone near me. But other than a couple who were walking their dog along the shoreline, there was no one. I must have imagined it.

As I started walking again, my head began to feel heavy and uncomfortable, like I had a virus or something. Then I heard the voice again.

You are walking very slowly. Perhaps you should pick up the pace. Aerobic exercise is very good for you.

Was I going crazy? Obviously the lack of friends and a social life on this holiday had affected me more than I realised.

'What's going on?' My words slipped out into the cold sea air. There was no one to hear them. I nearly freaked when an answer came back.

I should have thought that was obvious. I keep forgetting how limited humans are in their intelligence.

For the third time, I checked the beach to see if there was someone nearby. It was as empty as you would expect on one of the coldest July days ever. I was obviously sick, feverish maybe, definitely delusional.

I blamed my crazy parents, who had decided to come to the beach for the winter holidays because my mum was feeling stressed (she was a primary school teacher, enough said) and she wanted sea air, long beach walks and 'family time'. Temperatures were irrelevant, apparently. I loved my mum, but seriously?

I was nearly sixteen, and not happy about the several good parties I was going to miss. And the last thing I needed was to get ill on this holiday, especially since I wanted to be at the top of my game when I eventually got back to my friends and civilisation. I had plans.

No, you are not sick, far from it. You are now host to an alien. It does feel good to inhabit a body again. Where are we going, by the way?

'Who said that?' I was starting to lose it. This was way off the radar of normal.

2

An alien, a superior being that has become attached to you. I did say you were fortunate.

It took me several moments to process this, and even then I wasn't sure whether the voice was real or a figment of my imagination. 'Excuse me,' I said, feeling more than a little crazy, '*we* are not going anywhere. Get out, scram, and go back to your universe or whatever.'

The couple with the dog passed by and gave me a strange look. Oops, forgot I was talking out loud.

This was a bad dream, a very bad dream. I tried pinching myself to wake up.

I tried thinking what I wanted to say. *Go away.*

I cannot. The voice was unpleasantly smug. *I am stuck here inside you. Never mind, you will get used to me. Inhabiting an emotional adolescent female is not my idea of a perfect match either, you know. I would much prefer a surgeon, a biochemist, or even a politician. Politicians are always good for a laugh, with so much lying, backstabbing and Machiavellian manoeuvring. But I was released from the mothercloud over Queensland, and then fate and the wind currents brought me to you.*

'I don't believe this is happening,' I muttered aloud.

The voice continued as if it hadn't heard me. *You now have the benefit of 4,367 years of consciousness on this earth. My alien life, however, is barred from you.*

Even the most intelligent of your species would have difficulty in comprehending the complexity and richness of my superior race.

You're just a soap bubble, or maybe a piece of that awful pizza we had last night.

I thought that pizza was off. It must've been the mushrooms. I was seriously sick. I probably had a fever or something.

I started to jog up the beach. Maybe I could lose this annoying little voice if I went fast enough. Perhaps the wind would blow it away or the fresh air would make me feel better.

No, you are not sick, just a bit slow in understanding the situation. I will try again. There was a loud sigh and the voice continued. *I am an alien and you are my host. You may as well accept it. This run is invigorating, by the way. I am so glad you took my advice about exercise.*

Damn, it was still there. I slowed down, puffed. I'd reached the beach exit that led to our unit. I really hoped that whatever weird delusion I was having would end soon, but in the meantime I decided to play along with this voice in my head.

Okay, listen, I'm going home. No funny stuff. My parents are there and I don't want them to know anything about you. They'll think I'm crazy.

As a matter of fact, *I* thought I was crazy, too.

Not crazy, dear child, just enhanced. You now have the benefit of 4,367 years—

Yeah, yeah, heard it the first time. Just be quiet.

For a while everything seemed normal again. I didn't hear the voice and I assumed that whatever weird thing had happened to me on the beach was over. But the trouble with assumptions is they are just that— assumptions. Considering my luck these holidays, I should have known better.

At dinner I looked down at the plate of mushy broccoli and overcooked chicken. Mum had decided to cook to give us a change from all the takeaway meals we'd been having. My mother is lovely and means well, but, sadly, she hasn't realised she just can't cook. She does try, unfortunately.

After what happened on the beach I had less appetite than usual, so I tried my usual strategy. 'Mum, I've got a stomach ache, I can't really eat at the moment.'

Her face softened in concern. 'Again, dear?' she said. 'We really must have that checked. You seem to get stomach aches a lot lately.'

Dad looked at me suspiciously. 'You were fine this afternoon. Trouble with you is you don't have enough food going through your system. You need to eat more.'

I suppressed a groan. I'd heard all this before.

'I eat plenty, Dad. I just don't feel up to it at the moment. I think I'm coming down with something.' And after the afternoon's events, that wasn't exactly a lie.

Eat. The inner voice spoke firmly. *We need our strength.*

I gave a start and nearly dropped my fork.

'What's wrong?' Dad said.

'Nothing,' I said, giving him my wide-eyed innocent look.

The quicker I got out of there the better. I was just about to excuse myself from the table when my hand picked up the fork again and stabbed at a piece of broccoli. Without my wanting or meaning it to, the fork travelled towards my mouth. I felt like a puppet with strings. But what, exactly, was pulling them?

Even as I was still chewing, my hand went down and got a forkful of chicken.

Mum and Dad smiled at me, glad to see I was making an effort.

What's going on? I mentally telegraphed to whatever was doing this to me.

As a growing adolescent, nutrition is vitally important for your health. The voice was as annoying as ever.

I quickly looked at Mum and Dad to see if they'd heard the voice, but they seemed to be acting normally, showing no signs of noticing that their only child was going crazy.

What about free will here? I sent my thoughts to what, for lack of a better word, I was starting to think of as my alien. It was easier to call it that than what it really was—my delusional, nightmare madness brought about, I was sure, from a lack of socialising with my peer group and too many unhealthy sea breezes.

Let us just call this a benevolent dictatorship. I am acting in both our interests.

This was too much. I knew that coming to the beach on this holiday was a huge mistake. I finished my dinner quickly and escaped to my room.

It was the same thing all the rest of that evening. I wanted to stay up and watch a DVD. *It* wanted to go to bed early. I wanted to sneak a glass of wine and read my book in bed. *It* gave me a lecture on underage drinking. I forgot to brush my teeth, and I heard all about the importance of dental hygiene. I gave up, exhausted from my internal nanny, and went to bed.

Maybe, I thought hopefully, it'll be gone by tomorrow. The effect of bad mushrooms or whatever would surely have disappeared by then.

No such luck.

We are not going to sleep all day, are we?

I groaned and opened an eye. My alien was still there. It was dark, but my illuminated alarm clock said it was six am.

I am not getting up. It's the middle of winter, freezing cold, and besides, I'm on holiday.

Zip-a-dee-doo-dah, zip-a-dee-ay, my, oh my, what a wonderful day …

I closed my eye, put a pillow over my head and tried to shut out the cheery little voice singing inside me. *Stop! Stop!*

Let us go for a walk.

No. I thumped the pillow over my head.

Come on, it will be good for us. Think of the calories you will burn. You do not want to get fat, do you?

Shut up!

Silence finally. I breathed deeply and tried to settle down to sleep again. Bliss, I thought, peace at last. Just as I started drifting off, the alien spoke again in a huffy voice.

There is no need to be rude, you know.

Sigh. I removed the pillow, sat up in bed and focused. It was time for a serious talk. *Look, alien, what do you want?*

Ah, that is better, cooperation. Well, let us start with a nice run along the beach for an hour or so, and then we can come back and have some muesli with low-fat milk. If you have some green tea that would be ni—

That's not what I mean, I interrupted. *Why have you inhabited me? What's your long-term goal here? And when are you leaving?*

Hmm, did we not cover that yesterday?

No. You evaded my questions. I want answers, now, or I'll…

I had had enough and it was time for confrontation. I had a clever thought. *Or I'll have some Coco Pops, a packet of salt and vinegar chips, a Mars bar, and I'll wash all that down with a litre of Coke. Then I'll listen to some rap music on my iPhone, with the volume turned up so loudly I won't be able to hear a thing you say to me.*

You are not serious. A little joke, perhaps. Ha-ha. Oh, good one.

Actions spoke louder than words. I got out of bed and went to the kitchenette in our unit. Opening the cupboard, I took down the box of Cocoa Pops, shaking them purposefully.

Okay, okay, you win, the alien said. *I suppose a little information sharing would not go amiss.*

Good. I said and sat down on the sofa. In my parents' room I heard Dad snoring peacefully. Lucky him, I thought.

Well, go on, then, I said to the alien.

I had no choice about whom I inhabited. It was just luck, really. You were the first person I landed on. I suppose we should refine that process, but the premise behind random selection is that it enables us to get a true cross-section of Earth's population.

What if you hadn't landed on anyone? There's a lot of sand out there on the beach.

In that case I would have dissolved and evaporated back to the mothercloud. It happens all the time. That is why so many of us are released. Once I landed in the middle of the Kalahari Desert, and that was the fastest evaporation I had ever had, let me tell you.

So why do you want to inhabit humans?

It is not that we really want to merge with you. Good heavens, how would you feel if you had to be inside a dog, or, better analogy, a slug? No, it is just our purpose. We have to find out as much as we can about you and the best way to do that is to see firsthand how you live, how you think. We have been gathering information about you for eons. Well, 6,172 years, to be precise, give or take a few moons. Of course, that was when the first aliens arrived here. I came on the scene a couple of millennia later.

I didn't like the sound of this. *But why do you want to find out about us?*

We are expanding our knowledge of the universe. The more we learn about other worlds, the easier it will be to avoid the many mistakes and disasters those worlds make. Your Earth abounds in them, by the way.

So that's it? Nothing else? Just knowledge, huh? I wasn't convinced.

The alien sighed. *Is that not enough? No, I sense that it is not. All right, how about this. We are gathering knowledge for when we take over your world. Keep your friends close, and your enemies closer. I believe that is one of the sayings here.*

I heard a wicked chuckle inside my head.

Yup, I was right, I didn't like this at all. Smacked of all those nasty sci-fi movies where aliens, bugs, machines, et cetera, are poised to swoop down on Earth and eliminate us all. But one thing puzzled me.

You must have a lot of info about us by now. How come it's taken you soap bubbles so long?

I knew telling you anything was a mistake. If only I could have landed on a physicist or a nuclear scientist. They might have some idea of the scope and magnitude of this information.

This alien had a serious ego problem. *If that's the case, why don't you just evaporate and go back to the mothershi—*

Cloud, it interrupted. *Mothercloud.*

Whatever. Well, why don't you?

I thought I explained that yesterday. I cannot. I am bonded to you now.

Eeuw. *For how long?*

Let me see. You are fifteen, nearly sixteen, and the average lifespan of a Western Caucasian female is around eighty years, so that means it will be about sixty-five years. Oh well, it could be worse, I suppose. I will be able to guide you through these troublesome years with my superior knowledge. You might consider yourself quite fortunate, really. You have definitely got the better end of the deal.

No way! I'm not going to have you with me for the rest of my life. That's not happening, mister.

You have no choice.

There must be some way I can get rid of you.

Yes, there is.

Relief, big time. *How?*

When you die I will return to the mothercloud until it is time for me to be released to another human. You are my eighty-third human.

'Oh, God, kill me now,' I said aloud.

Not yet, dear, that is just your hormonal, adolescent propensity to overdramatise everything and indulge in meaningless emotional histrionics.

What?

You will get over it.

I groaned.

'Is that you, Zoe?' Mum called from my parents' bedroom. 'Why are you up so early?'

I needed some time to think, to plan, to plot. 'Just going for a run on the beach, Mum. Be back in a little while.'

'Okay, dear.'

I knew you would see it my way.

Over the next few days I tried everything I could think of to get rid of the alien inside me. I ate junk food and blasted music on my iPod that was too loud even for me. By the end of the holiday I had an aching head and had gained a kilo. But my invader was still there. I was beginning to realise that if this was a dream, it was a waking nightmare and there was no escape.

Even my parents began to notice there was something wrong with me.

'Are you all right, honey?' my mum asked on the last day. 'You don't look too well.'

And who would, I thought, with an alien inside them. But I answered, 'I'm okay.' I wondered what she would say if I told her the truth.

'This holiday doesn't seem to have done you much good,' she said. 'I thought it would be lovely and peaceful at the beach this time of year, without the crowds and everything. And the sea air, so fresh and clean. But you look pale and peaky. Perhaps you've picked up a bug or something.'

I nearly choked on my orange juice at that one.

'She's fine,' my dad said as he picked up his coffee cup. 'She'll perk up soon enough when we get home and she's with her friends.' He looked at me and winked.

Ordinarily I would have agreed with him. But I was sure that going home wouldn't solve the problem I had.

And I was right.

Chapter Two

On the first day of term my alien was sooo excited.

Ah, a place of learning. People to meet, books to read, knowledge to be gained. Is that not a wonderful thing?

If I had to be invaded by an alien, why couldn't it have been one that was a bit cooler? I set the record straight.

People to meet, yes. Books and knowledge are something else. I'm not a nerd, you know. I shifted my bag to the other shoulder and crossed the street to the bus stop. *And no funny business*, I told it. *Just stay in the background and let me get on with things. It's my life, you know.*

Correction, our lives, the alien said. *We are bonded now.*

I made a pucking sound. *Stop saying that*, I said.

I decided to walk to my friend Jas's bus stop so I could talk to her. I wasn't ready to confide in her yet, but maybe, at the right moment, I could tell her the truth and we could work together to get me out of this dilemma.

'Zoe!' She gave me a hug. 'It's so good to see you again. We really missed you at Sam's party.'

I grimaced. 'Don't remind me about everything I missed. The beach was such a drag. I hated it. I mean, who goes to the beach in winter? I couldn't even go swimming.'

Maybe that would've gotten rid of the alien. If I'd thought of that earlier I might even have braved the icy waves. I was willing to try just about anything at this point.

'Never mind,' Jas said, 'there's another get-together this weekend at Chelsea's place. You've *got* to go to this one. Everyone will be there.' She flicked her blonde hair over her shoulders. 'That is, everyone who counts.'

I knew she was telling the truth. Those were the only kind of parties Jas ever attended.

'I'll have to be super-persuasive about this one,' I said. 'Mum's not real keen on Chelsea since her party last term. Mum doesn't think Chelsea's mum is very responsible, not after she saw one of the boys drinking when she picked me up.' I rolled my eyes. 'Parents.'

Jas nodded sympathetically. 'I know.'

The bus pulled up and we got on. I nodded to a couple of friends, but Jas and I moved to the back where we could talk. I felt, rather than heard, my alien stirring inside me. I gave it a silent warning to be quiet. It seemed to work.

Jas filled me in on all the gossip that had happened over the holidays. It only made me more depressed to hear about everything I'd missed. And then I had a thought—if I hadn't gone on holiday I wouldn't have this stupid alien now. That really was a bummer.

When we got to school we had to go our separate ways. Jas had maths and I had English.

'Hey, Zoe,' she said before she left, 'why don't you tell your parents you're spending the night at my place? That way you can go to the party with me and come home with me, and they won't know a thing.'

I hesitated. I had never really lied to Mum and Dad before and it made me feel a bit uncomfortable. 'I'll think about it,' I said.

Jas shrugged. 'Whatever. See you later.'

I walked slowly to E block and my English class, thinking about Jas's idea. She was super-popular and at long last she considered me a friend. I didn't want anything to jeopardise that.

Forget it, Zoe. We are not going to that party and you are not going to lie to your parents. I simply will not allow it. My alien's voice was loud and clear in my head.

17

'You've got to be joking,' I said out loud. A few kids gave me weird looks, and I dodged behind a tree, breathing heavily and full of indignation. *Who the hell do you think you are, telling me what I can do?*

Very well, if you have to be reminded. I am now part of you, and the better part, I might add. I am not going to allow our body to be poisoned with alcohol and deafened by loud music, and our indigestion ruined with bad food, much less consort with unacceptable companions. And as for being deceitful to the ones who brought you into this world and looked after you, that is out of the question.

First of all, you interfering busybody, I don't drink. Well, except for the occasional glass of wine I've snuck from Mum and Dad, which didn't really count. And I'd only done that twice. I didn't get to drink it the third time— thanks to my annoying alien. Most of my friends' parents let them drink at home, unlike my uncool parents. Well, Chelsea's mum did anyway. But that was beside the point and it was definitely not information I was going to share with Mr Nosey Parker Alien.

Secondly, I said to my alien, *eating junk food and listening to cool music is part of being a teen so get over it. And thirdly, those so-called unacceptable companions happen to be my friends. And finally, they are* my *parents and not yours.*

If it was possible for a soap bubble to tut, this one did. The disapproval was so heavy it almost made me sick. The alien lapsed into a sulky silence for the rest of the day, which was fine with me.

Did I say sulky? I should have said ominous.

For the rest of the school week my alien was very quiet, almost well behaved. I only got two or three sermons a day on trivial stuff like watching *The Vampire Diaries* instead of the Discovery channel, copying Harry Crosby's chemistry homework, and pretending I had a stomach ache in maths because I hadn't studied for the test, things hardly worth mentioning.

But if that wasn't enough to warn me, I should have guessed that something was up when it let me drink a glass of Coke without a murmur of protest.

I did have a moment of guilt when I asked Mum if I could stay over at Jas's place on Saturday night.

She looked at me with her trusting brown eyes and said, 'Of course, dear, I know you must have missed her when we were away.'

Dad looked up from his newspaper. 'I suppose you'll stay up all night gabbing. Don't know why it's called a sleepover. Seems to me not much sleeping goes on.'

'Honestly, Dad, I'm not a child,' I complained.

His sharp eyes caught mine, and for a minute I thought he was going to say something else. But he just grunted and disappeared behind his paper again.

Are you not ashamed of yourself? My alien's tone was mega-disapproving.

I decided to ignore it as I bounced into my room to text Jas. No way was I going to miss yet another cool party.

I love Saturdays, usually. The whole weekend stretches ahead like a red liquorice string, you know, the kind that seems to last forever. Sometimes the liquorice breaks and sometimes it's gone before you know it, but when you first start eating it, the end seems a long way away.

This Saturday, though, was even more special. Chad Everett was going to be at the party. He was the hottest boy in our grade and every girl wanted him. He'd only come to our school at the end of last term, and so far he hadn't gone out with anyone.

So far. I wanted to change that status tonight.

I dressed in my old jeans and T-shirt, carefully packing the black lacy top I'd borrowed from Deb. Her parents weren't as uptight as mine about what she could and couldn't wear, but she couldn't go to the party because she had a cold. I put on my tight, black skinny jeans and the cool boots that went with them, and covered them with my PJs and a jumper. I knew Mum would insist on a jumper, and it was nice and bulky, hiding everything.

All went beautifully to plan. Mum dropped me off at Jas's with a minimum of fuss. No probs, not even from the alien. A great night loomed ahead.

'I'm mega-excited about tonight,' Jas said, as we got ready in her room. She pulled on a slinky, midnight blue top, exposing several centimetres of fake-tanned skin. Summer or winter made no difference to her; she always looked like she'd come back from a holiday on the Gold Coast.

'Me, too,' I said, shimmying into my top. It was a bit loose because Deb was a size up from me, but it was still way trendier than anything else I owned. I'd probably freeze, but I didn't care.

I ignored the exaggerated shivering sounds my alien was making inside me. *Do not forget your jumper*, it said.

As if. When I went to this much trouble to look good I wasn't going to cover up with a jumper that was bulky and totally dorky. I really needed some new clothes. Ones that didn't make me look about twelve.

Jas sat down at the mirror and took out her mascara, applying it carefully. I watched her closely, taking note of her technique, and then dug out the makeup bag I had carefully packed. I sat down beside her and started to apply my own makeup. For a few moments we were absolutely silent as we concentrated on making ourselves look fabulous—well, in my case, at least acceptable. Try as I might, I could never quite manage to look as hot as my friend.

I looked at my round baby face and sighed. What I really wanted was high cheekbones and a straighter nose, but there was only so much makeup could do. And tonight I seemed to have two left hands. When I tried to apply eyeliner my hand shook and it went on crooked. Mascara was impossible because I kept dropping the brush.

What was wrong with me tonight? In the end I gave up and settled for blush and lip gloss. Perhaps Chad wouldn't notice my slight imperfections. I'd have to dazzle him with my sparkling personality instead.

As if reading my thoughts, Jas said, 'I really want to look good tonight. Chad Everett's going to be there.'

My heart sank, but I wasn't surprised Jas was interested in Chad. Every girl in our grade had a crush on him. But her next words did take me aback.

'I've made up my mind and tonight's the night.' She turned to me, her now outlined eyes large and totally perfect, unlike my own. 'Chad's mine,' she said. 'I want you to keep the other girls away while I'm talking to him. You're good at that sort of thing, talking and everything.'

'I don't know if I can do that, Jas.' And what's more, I didn't want to. I wanted a chance to talk to Chad myself.

'Come on, what are friends for? Course you can.'

'What if Chad wants to talk to other people?' Like me, I thought.

She laughed. 'Once he's with me he won't want to. You know what I'm like with boys. Putty in my hands.' She shook her long, blonde silken hair back from her shoulders. 'It's almost too easy at times.'

Sadly, I did know what she was like with boys, but it had never bothered me before.

She rose and spritzed herself with Eau de Brittany.

'Can I borrow some?' I asked, confident of her answer. After all, we were practically best friends.

'Oh, Zoe, we don't want to smell the same. After all, we don't look the same.' Her laughter tinkled; it actually tinkled.

Some friend, my alien observed.

She really can be very nice, I answered in my head, though not with a hundred percent conviction.

23

Sometimes you had to work hard to keep Jas's friendship. And I had worked hard, so I wasn't giving it up any time soon.

I grabbed my bag and followed Jas outside where her mum was waiting in the car.

Where are the rest of your clothes? Where is your jumper? And by the way, have you looked at yourself in the mirror? Makeup is totally unnecessary at your age.

'Shut up,' I said to my soap bubble.

'What?' Jas looked at me in surprise.

Oops, I hadn't meant to say it out loud. 'Nothing,' I said. 'Come on, your mum's waiting.'

Chapter Three

At Chelsea's place, things were starting to buzz. Her mum had gone out for the evening, so there were no parents to supervise. How cool was that? Needless to say, my Neanderthal parents would have totally disapproved. Just as well I hadn't told them. I only felt a tiny twinge of guilt, which was getting smaller by the minute.

'Hey, Zoe, want a beer?' Marko asked, pulling one out of the esky by his feet. Marko was one of the ultra-cool boys who just managed to stay this side of trouble.

I didn't want to look like a complete nerd, so I thought maybe just this once I'd say yes. I held out my hand. 'Y—no, thanks.' Where did that come from?

My alien was suspiciously quiet.

As Marko shrugged and turned away from me, I confronted the interfering member of the fun police inside me. *Hey, you knew I was going to have a beer and you stopped me.*

Silence still. Smug silence.

Suddenly my clumsy attempts to put on makeup earlier one were starting to make sense. *And I bet you were behind all that trouble I had putting on makeup. Stop messing with me.*

You told me you did not drink, my alien said primly. *And you do not need makeup at your age. As for messing, I never make a mess. I am extremely tidy. You could learn a thing or two from me, especially by the look of your room this morning.*

You know what I mean. Don't interfere. There's such a thing as free will and all that. You aliens aren't meant to interfere with another species.

A nasty little laugh echoed inside me. After a few moments of headache-inducing cackles, my odious little alien recovered from whatever it thought was so funny.

Surely you know better than that by now. What a quaint idea. Where did you pick that up from, Star Trek*? When you have lived as long as I have you will realise the only thing you humans should be free to do is sleep. You haven't got a great history of using free will wisely, you know.*

Before the alien could go off on another rant, I cut it short. *Keep this up and I'll change my mind about that beer after all. I might even have two or three. You can't always stop me. I'll be more prepared for you next time.* No way was this bossy soap bubble going to ruin my night.

No need to get aggressive. I can compromise. Go on, have your junk food and listen to that ear-splitting music. You will be deaf and obese by forty, if you last that long. I am going to retire and reflect on the wisdom of the ages, which I have accumulated in my rich and varied existences.

'Yeah, beat it,' I said. This alien was wearing me out and the party had hardly even started.

'Sorry?' a voice said, and a warm tingly feeling spread through me.

I turned to see Chad Everett. He had a white T-shirt stretched across pretty good abs and his blond hair just skimmed over his summer-blue eyes. *Sigh.*

'Did you just tell me to beat it?' he asked.

'No, no, of course not,' I babbled. I really needed to control that speaking-my-thoughts-out-loud thing. Damn that alien.

'You're Zoe, right?' he said, and took a step closer.

God, he smelled nice. And he knew my name. 'Yeah, hi.' The words were barely a whisper and I really couldn't think of another thing to say.

'I'm Chad. I think we're in history class together.' He gave me a smile that had the peculiar effect of making my knees go weak.

'I know.' Everything inside me froze. Now that the big moment had come to speak with Chad, I couldn't think of a thing to say other than one or two syllables. Great.

My alien gave a long, bored sigh. *Ask him a question. Talk about your teacher or about what you learnt in history. Honestly, I do not know how you have lived these fifteen years without me.*

'Hey, that Mr Baxter, he's so boring, isn't he?' Lame, but the best I could do.

'Yeah,' Chad said, 'no wonder Jonesy fell asleep in class on Wednesday. Remember how he nearly fell off his chair?'

We laughed. Chad Everett and I actually laughed together.

'So, have you tried out for any of the school teams?' I asked, getting into my stride.

'Yeah, the footy team,' he said. 'I played union at my old school, but I can play league, too.'

Of course he could. I wasn't exactly sporty, but I could pretend that I at least knew something about football.

'What position do you play?'

'Do you want a drink?'

We both spoke at the same time and then laughed.

'You go first,' he said. Such a gentleman.

'I asked what position you played,' I said, 'but sure, I'd love a Coke.' Chad getting me a drink meant he had to come back to me. And that was absolutely fine.

'Oh, there you are.' A familiar voice cut through the air like an interfering commercial in *Gossip Girl*.

Jas moved between us with precision and determination, but not without giving me a look and a raised eyebrow. Then she turned her back on me and laid a hand on Chad's arm.

'Hi, Chad, I've been looking everywhere for you. No need for you to be hidden away in a corner. I know absolutely everyone here, and so many people want to meet you.'

I had to take a step back or risk having my foot pierced by Jas's spike heels. She was so subtle, my friend.

'Oh, hi Zoe,' she said over her shoulder and then turned back to Chad.

'That's okay,' he said to Jas. 'I think I know most people here.'

She gave a shake of her hair over her shoulders and said in her most persuasive voice, 'Oh well, then I want to get to know you better. There, I said it. You saw through me, didn't you?'

She gave a very irritating laugh. Irritating to me. Chad didn't seem to mind it.

'Come on, let's grab a drink and I'll tell you about everything and everyone you need to know in order to survive East Valley High.' Jas linked her arm through his and led him away as if I didn't exist.

To his credit, Chad did look back at me and smile. Sweet, but I knew he wouldn't be back. Looked like I'd have to get my own Coke.

She's very predatory, isn't she?

For once I agreed with my alien. But then it continued and spoiled the moment.

She displays all those qualities that my species admires in you lesser creatures. She is ruthless, determined and a born survivor. Perhaps this party has not been so bad after all. It is always so interesting, observing humans.

Whose side are you on, anyway?

What an unnecessary question. Ours is a mutually beneficial relationship, although more beneficial to you than me.

Whatever. I didn't feel like wasting time arguing.

Naturally, within five minutes I could see that Chad was totally focused on Jas and had forgotten me. She was using every trick she had and it was working. Normally, it didn't bother me. In fact, I used to admire her. Most of the boys she liked, like the jocks, the popular guys, weren't that interested in me anyway. I didn't care. Not much, anyway. But Chad was different. I really wanted to get to know him. But now the only way I could hang out with him was as the best friend of the girl he was really interested in.

I was already starting to be over this party. But I wasn't quite ready to call it quits, as I realised when I heard that irritating inner voice again.

Should we not be going home now?

It was quarter to ten. *Are you joking? Just how many parties have you gone to?* Wrong question.

Hmmm, let me think now. It is just as well I have hyperthymesia.

What?

I apologise, I forgot about your limited vocabulary. It means I have an exceptional memory. I have inhabited eighty-three people and I remember almost everything that happened while I was with them.

Pause.

The number of parties I have attended, including this one, which is not high on my list of enjoyable events, is 2,032. Apuleius wasn't much of a partygoer, but he was a brilliant scholar. Naturally, many of his theories came from me. But then, oh dear, Count de Vere made up for it. Such a wit. After the French Revolution we escaped to London, and what a time we had. We drank only the best champagne, although I am normally averse to alcohol, especially underage drinking. This was said in a warning tone. *However, I did feel it incumbent upon me to experience the full gamut of human experiences. Not that I tasted it. I am incapable of that. But I did feel the after-effects.*

Giggle. My alien actually giggled.

And then there were the Christmas parties held at Balmoral. Unfortunately my host person was only a lowly servant, but I still managed to see and hear such a lot. However, it was short-lived as he died when he was twenty. Just as well, since the servant's life was rather tiring on me. And then there was—

Enough already, I get it. You've been to a few parties. So you can put up with this one for a while longer. Suck it up, bubble.

Such crude language. You have no appreciation of and no gratitude for all the knowledge and guidance I can impart.

Gratitude? Seriously? What have you done except make my life miserable? If you were as smart as you say, and if you really wanted to help, you'd tell me how to get Chad Everett interested in me. But you're incapable of doing anything except talk, talk, talk. You're just an invisible bubble with an over-inflated ego.

I sat down in a chair in the corner and took a sip of my Coke. Other than a few microseconds with Chad, I'd hardly spoken to anyone in the room. That was partly because I

32

felt down, and partly because my alien wouldn't shut up and I didn't want to look weird talking to myself. If this was how things were going to be from now on, my life was as good as over, at fifteen and three-quarters. Great.

Silence. No wonder they say it's golden. I leaned back in the chair and closed my eyes.

Well, I must say it is a challenge.

I knew it was too good to last.

However, I do love a challenge. Even when it involves an adolescent female of limited experience and … I am sorry to say it, my dear, but also limited intellectual curiosity.

Gee, thanks, you sure are smooth with the compliments.

But with my guidance there might be some hope for improvement.

Yippee. What are we going to do now? Go for a jog, or make a green smoothie? I can't wait.

Certainly not, it is far too late and too dangerous for a jog. And while a green smoothie does sound delicious it might give you indigestion on top of that Coke. Oh, I see. Sarcasm. It really is the lowest form of wit.

Maybe it wasn't too early to go home.

Now listen to me, the alien said. *That is, if you really want that boy to pay attention to you.*

I looked over to where Chad was standing. Next to him, of course, was Jas, arm through his and with her body pressed close. But she didn't look too pleased. Surrounding them was a group of girls, three or four at least. I could hear their high-pitched laughter from where I sat in the corner. No way was I going to compete with that many girls.

Jas looked over and caught my eye. She nodded meaningfully at the girls around Chad and frowned. I knew what she wanted. She wanted me to go over and somehow break up the group.

'Hey Zoe, what are you doing over there? Come and join us,' she called, and waved me over.

Normally I would have rushed over and tried to do exactly what she wanted—normally, but not this time. I was over this party, and I was sick of obeying Jas's orders. So I just shook my head and smiled.

Good for you, my alien said approvingly. *Now tell her you are waiting for someone.*

But I'm not.

Do you want my help or not? Just do it.

Bossy, much. 'I'm waiting for someone,' I called to Jas.

She raised her eyebrows. Then, putting her hand on Chad's arm, she walked towards me, pulling him with her. Only Jas could get away with that. The girls trailed after them.

Jas stood in front of me, frowning. 'Who?' she said.

34

Tell her an acquaintance of your cousin who is in town for the weekend.

'A guy my cousin knows. He's just here for the weekend.'

Jas looked at me suspiciously. 'You never mentioned him before.'

'No, I didn't.'

Another frown and then she turned her back on me. She wasn't happy with me. Too bad I had to sleep at her place tonight. This alien had better come up with a good plan.

Now what? I asked.

It is the oldest trick in the book. Maria de Silva used it to get the Earl of Valencia interested in her and it has been used so many times it is almost cliché. You need to awaken the natural human male instinct for competition. You need to make Chad jealous.

Oh yeah, and how's that going to happen?

I agree it is a challenging prospect. I scanned the available males in the room and there are no prospects that would match up to that boy over there. You have set your sights high. Especially as you are average in looks and your personality is a little ...

What? This health-conscious alien was about to realise just how much junk food I could eat. I might even have that beer after all. I was ready to do anything to annoy it as much as it annoyed me. I'd worry about its lectures and the kilojoules later.

It must have suspected it was on dangerous territory. *You are just a little quiet,* it added quickly, *at least with boys. I am sure you have hidden depths and are probably going to grow into your looks. After all, while you may only look twelve now, by the time you are forty, looking younger than your age will be a great advantage.*

You can stop with the compliments now.

Anyway, there are no males here who are attractive or convincing enough to make this Chad boy jealous. And besides, how would we ever get any of them to pretend to be interested in you?

Gee, thanks.

No need to thank me yet, but you will before the night has ended. You have no idea of the sacrifice I am about to make. I will have to step in. I cannot think of any other way around it.

What do you mean? My suspicions were on high alert.

Big sigh. *I will have to materialise. I hardly ever do this and it is so uncomfortable. But you have set me a challenge and I am determined to rise to it.*

Materialise? What do you mean? I had a feeling I wasn't going to like this.

Take a physical form, of course.

You can do that? Why didn't you say so before now? Thoughts of escaping my alien inhabitant were beginning to form. *Hang on, you're not going to be some sort of bug or creepy lizard thing, are you? Because that would definitely not be helpful.*

Certainly not. As interesting as insects and amphibians are, I do realise they are not totally attractive to the human race in sexual terms.

Euwwww.

I shall become a sixteen-year-old boy, and by doing so will outshine everyone in this room, naturally.

I not only had a hard time believing this but I was a little worried in case something went dreadfully wrong. What if my alien's idea of attractive was different to everyone else's? What if it forgot which era we were living in and came dressed as a caveman or some guy from the eighteenth century? What if its spell or whatever went wrong and it came back as something else? Creepy thought.

There were so many what-ifs racing through my mind that I couldn't keep up with them. And, more importantly, how was this supposed to help me?

Sensing my doubts, the alien tried to reassure me.

Do not worry. It will be fine. And when I do materialise, I will be so attentive to you that Chad and every other girl in the room will notice. You will be the envy of all. Chad will be filled with the competitive urge that all male humans seem to feel when they encounter another male who is a challenge to them. Testosterone has a lot to answer for.

So did this alien. I was suspicious. *How come you can do this if you're supposed to be with me forever?* I repressed a shudder.

Not forever, just your lifetime, which will be infinitesimally short compared to mine. But to answer you, even if I materialise we are still bonded. I cannot go very far without you. It will be like a dog on a leash—a long leash, but a leash just the same.

I couldn't help smirking. *So you'll be a pet, like a dog or something?*

Actually, it is the other way around, which I thought would be obvious, even to you.

Ignoring the insult, I thought for a moment and then smiled. I was going to do my best to make sure this little puppy escaped. *Okay, let's do this thing.*

Chapter Four

*G*o outside and look at the sky. I work better in the outdoors. Besides, we don't want anyone else to see this.

I couldn't agree more with my alien. I was too worried about what might happen.

Getting up, I negotiated my way through the crowd and went to the door, hoping no one would notice me. No worries there. I could have been invisible.

Once outside, I stood on the path. Music and laughter floated out of the house, and there wasn't another soul in sight. I shivered in the cold and hugged myself to keep warm.

Let's just get on with it. I was still wondering if this was a good idea.

Very well, close your eyes.

Dramatic, much. I closed my eyes and waited. And waited. *Hurry up. Get a move on.* Gradually, I began to feel lighter inside. I hadn't felt this good since … before that soap bubble inhabited me.

'Amazing. I've forgotten how strange it feels to have a body,' an unfamiliar voice said beside me.

I turned and looked at the stranger. Oh. My. God.

Longish dark hair framed a face with cheekbones that could have cut glass, and his lips were … McDreamy. He was tall, over six feet, and while he wasn't built like a rugby-league centre forward he still looked pretty good in his black T-shirt. Intense, dark eyes looked down at me. And did I mention those lips, those very kissable lips?

Eeuw! What was I thinking?

'You scrubbed up well,' I said.

'I presume you mean that my male beauty is dazzling. I told you so,' he said, and smiled. That smile revealed perfect teeth and made my knees weak. Also, his voice was so different to how I had imagined it. I thought he would sound like that annoying robot in *Star Wars*, the one that was always worrying. Yes, I'm a science-fiction nerd, which I totally blame on my dad. I think he had me watching *Star Wars* when I was a baby.

My alien's voice was deep, sexy even, but the way he spoke was something else and it completely ruined the image he presented.

I looked up at him. 'You can't talk like that, you know. You'll sound like a weirdo, which you are, but if people *think* you're a weirdo it kind of defeats the purpose.'

He shrugged. 'I studied the voice and speech patterns of everyone here while you were engulfed in a wave of self pity, and I don't think we'll have any problems with me sounding weird.'

'Jeez, I see you haven't lost your charm.' I thought my sarcasm was obvious, but apparently not, as his next words proved.

'Hmm, I can see a problem.' He looked down at me, his brow creasing. 'How unlike me not to have foreseen this,' he said. 'You'll have to promise me one thing.'

'What?' I was curious.

'You can't fall in love with me.'

I was speechless for a moment. Then all the words I wanted to say tried to tumble out at once. 'You can't be … you're joking … you're an …'

He put his hands on my arms and I hated the fact that it felt kind of nice. Then he spoke again. 'I know I'm irresistible, and I can see that you're smitten already. But it just won't do. When I dematerialise again it will be … awkward.'

I moved away, lifted my chin and gave him what I hoped was a death stare. 'I'm not in the slightest danger of falling in love with you, not in this universe or any other. You are without doubt the biggest egomaniac I have ever met in my entire life. Not to mention irritating, sanctimonious, insensitive and totally unable to read human emotions. I don't even like you. As a matter of fact, I loathe you.'

'See, already I've improved your vocabulary.' He gave me a slightly crooked smile, which, damn him, made him look even more attractive.

I gave an exclamation of disgust and only just stopped myself from stamping my foot. 'I *knew* this was a bad idea,' I said.

'Zoe, what are you doing out here?'

I turned to see Jas, and with her, Chad, with his arm over her shoulder. God, she was quick. I saw her look at my alien, and while her jaw didn't exactly drop she definitely looked surprised.

'Chad and I came out to get some fresh air,' she said. 'It's so stuffy in there, with so many people. So, who is this?' She moved away from Chad, making his arm drop to his side, and gave my alien a bright smile. Lions and tigers had nothing on Jas when it came to being predatory.

'Parties usually do have a lot of people, Jas,' I said. But Jas was yet another person who didn't get my sarcasm. I must be losing my touch, I thought.

'This is my cousin's friend,' I said. And then I stopped. I was totally at a loss for a name.

'Hi, I'm Orion,' my alien said, and shot out a hand.

Jas had that deer-in-the-headlights-look as she shook his hand. 'I'm Jas, and this is Chad.'

Chad looked annoyed, but he made an effort to be polite. 'Hi,' he said. He didn't even appear to see me; such was the power of Jas. I really hoped this crazy alien's plan worked.

'Orion, what an unusual name,' Jas gushed. 'Is that foreign or something? It really suits you.'

'Orion' laughed a sexy laugh and Jas's fake eyelashes fluttered. 'My parents were really into astronomy,' he said. 'That's where they got the name.'

'Astronomy?' Jas looked bewildered.

'Orion is a constellation, Jas. You know, a star pattern in the sky,' I said, trying to make it simple for her. She was far from dumb, but my alien had obviously affected her brain—well, his looks had, anyway.

'Oh, I see.' Her face broke out in a smile. 'How original.'

I could sense Orion reading the situation quickly. 'But my friends call me Rion.'

'I would love to be your friend, Rion.' Jas had the flirt factor turned up high.

I glanced over at Chad, who was looking more than a little peeved. I tried to smile encouragingly at him, as if to signal the message: *I wouldn't treat you like that, Chad.* But he only had eyes for Jas.

'And I'd love you to be my friend as well,' Mr McDreamy Traitor said to Jas.

Maybe if Rion did his job and flirted with me, Chad *would* start to notice me. After all, that was the plan.

I grabbed Rion's hand. 'Come on, let's go inside,' I said, 'it's freezing out here.'

He turned his dazzling self to me and put his arm around my shoulders, pulling me close. 'So sorry,' he said, 'you should've said so sooner.'

I had the satisfaction of seeing both Jas and Chad look surprised. I snuggled into Rion and looked up into his face with what I hoped was an adoring smile.

As we walked away, he quirked an eyebrow and looked down at me. 'Perhaps you should've listened to me, Zoe, and worn a cardigan after all. Your nose has gone red with the cold.'

For a nanosecond I had felt comfortable with that arm around me. But this last remark reminded me that underneath that rock-star exterior was the same annoying soap bubble.

'Orion?' I whispered. 'Seriously? That's the best name you could come up with?' I shook his arm off me.

He opened the door for me. 'It seemed apt. It's the constellation where my home is situated.'

'Oh.' I hadn't thought of him having a home before. I hadn't even thought of him as an individual; more like some awful disease I'd caught. I caught a look of sadness in his eyes.

'Do you miss it?' I asked him. 'Your home?'

For the first time it hit me that my alien was real, and not just a figment of my overactive imagination. Without thinking, I put my hand on his arm. But that sad look disappeared as soon as he stepped into the crowded room.

'Sympathy, Zoe,' he said mockingly. 'Do be careful.'

I turned around to face him. 'What are you talking about?'

'Smitten, I told you it would happen.' His face broke out into a wide grin. 'I'm that irresistible.'

It was amazing how quickly my sympathy evaporated. I gave him a sharp nudge in the ribs with my elbow.

'Ow,' he said, in a very un-alien-like manner. 'What was that for?'

'Pain,' I said, 'remember it. That's what'll happen if you make wisecracks like that again, buddy.'

He straightened up and said in a patronising tone, 'You know I'm doing you a favour here, right?'

'That remains to be seen.'

'Zoe! I haven't had a chance to catch up with you all night.'

Chelsea, who was throwing the party, was making a beeline for us. Dark, straightened hair, pencil-thin eyebrows, and heels that added at least five centimetres to her height, she was almost as perfect as Jas. Again I wondered how I managed to get into the same group as these people. Chelsea and I were friendly-ish, but not close pals. Because Jas was my friend, Chelsea had to put up with me. But she didn't usually greet me so enthusiastically. I suspected her welcome had more to do with Rion than me.

Chelsea gave me a hug, and the familiar scent of Eau de Brittany enveloped me. Did she and Jas have the same perfume, or was Jas just more generous with Chelsea than me? She definitely looked more like Jas with her cool clothes, expert makeup and a figure that, well, put it this way—she *had* a figure. I, sadly, did not. A ruler had more curves than me.

Stepping back from her, I tried to lose that depressing thought.

'So, you brought a friend,' Chelsea said, turning to Rion.

He gave her a megawatt smile. 'Hi, I'm Rion. I'm a friend of Zoe's cousin. I hope you don't mind that I crashed your party.'

As if. There were way more girls than guys at Chelsea's party, and Rion was not exactly the ugliest of boys.

'Of course not,' she said, and giggled. 'Gee, I had no idea Zoe's cousin had such cute friends.' Flutter-flutter.

'Zoe has some pretty cool friends, too,' Mr Smoothie said, and gave her another smile.

Chelsea giggled again. 'Come with me and I'll get you a drink.'

'A Coke would be great, thanks,' Rion said.

A *Coke*—and after all his lectures to me. I wasn't going to let him get away with that. 'I thought you said soft drinks were really bad for you, Rion. All those chemicals and sugar, wasn't that what you said?'

'Well, this is a party, Zoe. And isn't that what kids our age do, eat junk food and listen to loud music?' There was that infuriating lifted eyebrow again. 'But you have a point. Make it a diet Coke, please, Chelsea. I'm in training.'

I glared at him, but Chelsea was oblivious to me. 'Really? What sport do you play?'

'Several, but I'm training for …' He was at a loss.

'Cricket,' I said, forgetting it was winter. Then I added, 'They're getting in shape for the summer season.'

Chelsea continued to ignore me. 'I'm very into sport,' she said to Rion. 'I'm on the cheerleading squad.' Flick of the hair.

'It doesn't surprise me in the least,' he answered. 'You look very … athletic.'

I only just stopped myself from making gagging noises.

'You should come and watch a game sometime,' Chelsea said, edging closer to him. 'Our footie team is the best.'

'He's only here for the weekend,' I said. Hopefully no more than a few hours, I thought. Rion was attracting more attention than I'd expected, and I only hoped we could pull this off without making a mistake.

'Oh no, really? Where are you from?' Chelsea looked at him all wide-eyed, definitely interested now.

'The Gold Coast,' I said, trying to be helpful.

'The Sunshine Coast,' he said at the same time.

Chelsea looked puzzled. Jeez, I thought, if she really knew where he was from she'd look more than puzzled.

I stepped on his foot, signalling him to be quiet and let me handle this. He winced but didn't say a word.

'Rion's parents are divorced, and he spends some time with his dad on the Gold Coast and some time with his mum on the Sunshine Coast.' I felt rather pleased with myself for coming up with such a clever answer.

Chelsea pulled a sympathy face. 'I know all about that. Mum's divorced, several times, actually. But I see my real dad sometimes. He lives in Sydney. Come on, Rion, let's get you that drink.'

'No worries, I've got it.' Jas came drifting over with a beer in her hand, which she shoved at Rion.

'Rion doesn't drink,' I said.

'I'm in training,' he said again, giving the beer back to Jas. 'But thank you anyway.'

'Rion is really against underage drinking,' I said. 'He doesn't approve of people who drink.' I looked pointedly at the beer in Jas's hand.

Rion gave me a look. 'It's not the people I don't approve of, Zoe, but the practice. I'm into a healthy lifestyle, as you know.'

'Just telling it like it is,' I said, meeting his eyes. 'Wouldn't want anyone to get the wrong impression here.'

'I'm so into healthy living,' Jas said, as she slid the untouched beer onto a table next to her. 'I did the green diet once. You know, the one where you only eat green vegetables. I lost five kilos on that and felt so good.' She put her hand on her waist and stuck out her chest, not so subtly showing off her terrific figure.

'A limited diet might be all right for short-term weight loss,' Rion said, 'but for overall health a balanced diet with a large proportion of fruit and vegetables is best.'

Then he launched into a spiel on the relative merits of different diets, and soon had the crowd—the female crowd, at least—transfixed. Any other guy would have sounded like a complete geek, but Rion, looking like a cross between the lead singer in a boy band and a star in a vampire movie, soon had a bunch of groupies around him, hanging onto his every word. I had heard his monologues on a healthy diet too many times to be impressed.

I stepped back away from the group and found myself standing next to Chad Everett, who was looking abandoned and downcast.

I was very good at comforting people, so I said, 'Hey, Chad, how you going?'

He smiled and shrugged.

Awkward pause. Why couldn't I think of something scintillating and sparkly to say?

'Your cousin's friend seems to be very popular,' he said.

'Yeah, Rion sure loves to talk.' And lecture, and preach ... I could write a book about that, I thought.

'You know him well?'

'I only met Rion recently.' I wondered what Chad would say if I told him the real story of how I met Rion. He'd probably freak out. 'But he's very friendly and we get on really well.' I should've crossed my fingers behind my back when I made that statement, such a lie it was. But I remembered my agenda to make Chad jealous so he'd think I was interesting, desirable and even cool.

'Oh,' Chad said.

Silence. What had happened to that promising start we'd had when he first came to the party? I'd thought for sure we'd had something going, or at least could have. But I knew the answer and it was just one word: Jas.

I tried again. I tried to shake my brown hair over my shoulders, but because it was chin length it came right back and flicked me in the eyes. Ouch.

'Yes, we've met a few times when I've visited my cousin,' I said, 'and we really get on. That's why he's here, to see me. He says I'm one of the most interesting, attractive girls he's ever met.' Maybe I was laying it on a bit thick, but that seemed to work for Jas.

'Rion's like, your boyfriend, then?' Chad said it as if it didn't matter to him in the least one way or another. So not good. Maybe I needed to drop a hint or two.

'Oh no, no, no,' I said, 'at least not yet. I like him, but, you know, there's a lot of nice boys here, too.'

I gave him my most dazzling smile and tried for a careless laugh, which came out as a high-pitched giggle. Chad gave me a weird look, which was not what I was going for. I really needed to brush up on my flirting skills.

'Jas seems to like him, too,' he said.

Jas had put her hand possessively on Rion's sleeve and was laughing at something he said.

'Jas likes lots of people,' I said. It was definitely time to change the subject. 'So, Chad, how are you finding our school?' Okay, it was the lamest question in the world, but I couldn't think of anything else.

He made an effort to drag his eyes away from Jas and look at me. He really did have the most beautiful blue eyes. 'It's okay. People are very friendly.' He smiled. At last we were getting somewhere. 'Although I still miss my old friends,' he added.

'Anyone in particular? Like, did you have ... a girlfriend or anything?' I couldn't stop myself from asking.

He hesitated a moment and then said, 'Yeah, but we broke up before I moved. She looked a lot like Jas.'

Okay, another stupid question, but also a lightbulb moment. So that was why he liked Jas, as well as the other obvious reasons. She reminded Chad of his ex. He probably still had feelings for her, so what chance did I have? For a moment I felt dejected, but then I decided to take a chance.

'Well, then, nothing like a change,' I said. Flutter-flutter. My eyelashes weren't long, but I did the best I could

'Is there something in your eye?' Chad asked.

'What do you mean?'

'You keep blinking,' he said, moving away from me.

My hand dropped loosely to my side. 'I'm fine.' I was annoyed. I wasn't cut out for this. Obviously I needed help.

I looked over to where Rion was still the centre of attention. Wasn't he supposed to be helping me? 'I think I'll go and rescue Rion,' I said.

'Good idea,' Chad said, perking up and sounding more cheerful than he had since I'd been talking to him.

Chapter Five

I pushed my way through the girls and stood in front of Rion. 'Hey, Rion, you want some food? I think there's pizza here somewhere.'

I tried to signal him with my eyes that we needed to get moving on our original agenda. If only we had that mind thingy going on right now, I thought. I could tell him how I felt about all this needless flirting with the wrong people. Not that I wanted him to flirt with me, or anything, but hey, it was part of the plan. And I was getting desperate.

'Pizza? Oh, Rion wouldn't eat anything like that. Think of the carbs.' Jas gave an elaborate shudder as if I'd offered him arsenic or something.

'No, Rion's into paleo,' Chelsea said.

'I thought he was vegetarian,' one of the other girls said.

'I think it was vegan,' said another.

Rion just stood there, lapping up all the attention. His ego was even bigger than I thought.. I knew he was vain and opinionated, but I hadn't realised he would get away with it just because he looked hot.

I was sick of subtle. 'I need to talk to you *now*, Rion.' I grabbed his arm and pulled him away. 'And Chelsea, I think I heard a car pulling up outside. It's probably parents. Maybe you should tell the guys to put the beer away. Jas, honey, mascara.' I pointed to my eyes.

Chelsea was immediately alert, and Jas's hand went to her eyes. Both girls disappeared quickly. Why wasn't I this good with the opposite sex?

Rion seemed to snap out of it. 'Zoe, where have you been all evening?'

'About two metres away from you,' I said. 'Observant, aren't you?' I dragged him over to a corner.

'I was preoccupied.'

'So I saw. What did you think you were doing?' I stepped back from him and crossed my arms over my chest.

Rion looked at me in surprise. 'Why, helping you, of course.'

'Helping me? How?' I really was bewildered.

'By distracting the other girls so you could talk to that boy. What's his name again? Oh yes, Chad. How did you get on? Not too well, by the look of it, otherwise you wouldn't be here with me.'

Trust my friendly little soap alien to make me feel better.

'Don't feel too bad, Zoe. I told you Chad was out of your league. Why not try that boy over there? He looks more your type.' He was pointing at Harry Crosby, who was eating pizza and trying to look as if it didn't matter that no one was talking to him. 'Mind you, he does look as if he suffers from low self-esteem and body-image problems, but between the two of us we could do him a lot of good.'

I mentally counted to ten before I said or did something I regretted. 'That's not why you're here,' I said as calmly as I could, 'so leave poor Harry out of this. I actually do talk to him sometimes. He's a friend, but he's not … boyfriend material. And, by the way, you're not doing anything for my self-esteem either.'

I felt a bit guilty about Harry. I knew I should have said hello to him before now. I gave him a wave and he smiled back.

'But I've already improved you. You express yourself very well now, thanks to me. And I don't mean to be harsh, but perhaps you're not girlfriend materi—'

I took a step closer to him and stuck my finger in his chest. 'Don't say it,' I warned.

He backed off and put his hands up. I was beginning to notice my alien didn't like physical confrontation. 'Calm down, Zoe, your aggressive behaviour isn't your most admirable trait. What do you want me to do?'

'Stick with the plan. Refocus. You were supposed to make Chad jealous so he would think I was great.'

'Instead, you're jeal—okay, I won't say it, but you know it's true.' He looked at me with a smug expression.

'I am *not* jealous. Unlike the girls who were hanging onto your every word, I know exactly what you're really like. This pretend body you're occupying doesn't change a thing.'

'It's not pretend,' he said. It's quite real, actually. I can eat, drink, run—'

'Can you feel pain?' I tried my own eyebrow lifting.

He got the point. He took another step back. 'Where's Chad?'

We looked around and saw him over in the corner talking to some of the guys. Apparently they were more interesting to him than I was, because at least he was laughing at what they were saying.

'Okay, I'm going to put my arm around you. No hitting, right?' Rion looked at me anxiously.

I rolled my eyes. 'Let's get this over with.'

His arm snaked around my shoulders and I found myself nestling into the contours of his body. Okay, it didn't feel altogether terrible. If only it was Chad doing this and not my alien. We walked over to where some of the boys were standing.

'Hi, guys,' I said. 'This is Rion. He's just visiting for the weekend.'

'Hey, mate,' Con Adams said.

The other guys, including Chad, gave him a nod. Then they all started talking about footy, and I was surprised at how much my alien knew. A couple of the girls drifted over, and one of them suggested dancing, looking pointedly at Rion. What was I, invisible?

Chelsea put on some music.

'Come on,' Rion said, pulling me towards a tiny free space. 'I want to dance with the hottest girl in the room.' It was all I could do not to roll my eyes at that one.

He grinned down at me as we started to dance. I slid my eyes sideways towards Chad, who looked surprised, as did everyone else in the room.

'You're a convincing liar,' I shot back as we moved to the music. Rion was, surprisingly, not totally uncoordinated.

'I'm quite proficient at everything, and technically speaking I wasn't lying. Your temperature is a little elevated,' he said.

'Thanks, buddy, it matches your ego.'

'Don't complain. At least it got their attention. Oh good, the music has slowed. I was hoping it would.'

He pulled me into his arms and I let myself sink into his broad, rock-hard chest. For a moment I closed my eyes and let myself imagine it was Chad who was holding me. Rion felt good, and I might even have been just a tiny bit attracted to him if he'd been a real person. I could even feel his heart beat—his fake, pretend heart that seemed so real.

I allowed my arms to wrap themselves around his neck, and without thinking I found my thumb caressing the back of his neck. I felt a shiver go through him. Hey, did I do that? I was beginning to wonder what other reactions I could get from him, just purely out of intellectual curiosity, when I remembered my purpose.

I looked over to see where Chad was. To my surprise he was still watching us. Great, the plan was working.

'Okay, I'm going to dip you,' Rion said. 'Are you ready for it?'

Before I could answer, he dipped me low, like they do on *Dancing with the Stars*, and then swung me up again. Then he twirled me around and swung me back into his arms. I looked up into his dark eyes, which were shining. Somewhere I heard a little clap, but it was obviously for my alien and not me.

'Wow,' I said, 'where did you learn that?'

'One of my previous hosts was a dancing instructor. I picked up a thing or two, but I've never physically danced before. I didn't realise how exhilarating it is.'

'Not bad, mister,' I said. 'What other moves have you got?'

'Praise, Zoe? How unusual,' he said, as he dipped me again.

We did a few more dips and swings, and I was actually having fun when Jas sidled up to us. She was dancing with Chad, of course.

'We're cutting in,' she said. 'Come on, time to change partners.'

Rion moved smoothly to her and they were away. Chad and I stood together awkwardly, looking at each other. This was what I'd wanted, wasn't it? He held out his arms and we danced slowly. He wasn't a terrible dancer, and he was trying to be polite and all, but his eyes kept drifting towards Jas and Rion. He wasn't holding me closely; you probably could have driven a truck in the space between us.

I looked up at him. He was just as gorgeous as ever, but I knew that even if I did backflips naked he still wouldn't notice me. All that scheming and plotting for nothing. As long as Jas was in sight, I simply didn't exist for him.

After the dance, he drifted away from me and I made no attempt to stop him. Instead, I moved to the table and took a large slice of pizza. What difference did it make if I got fat? No boy would ever notice me. Even Harry had disappeared. Maybe he'd gone home, and who could blame him?

I was halfway through my third bite when I had an idea, a *brilliant* idea. Rion was still dancing, only now with Chelsea instead of Jas, who had moved back to a much-relieved Chad. Maybe I could still get *something* out of this little venture, even if it wasn't Chad.

Rion had said that we were still connected, even though he had materialised. I wasn't sure if I believed that, but I was going to test it out. It would be so good to be rid of him once and for all. I would be free again.

I looked over at him; he was totally engrossed in being the star. No one would notice if I left. Maybe if I went far enough away I could break the bond between us. I moved to the door slowly so he wouldn't notice me. Then I slipped out.

I'd forgotten how cold it was, but what did it matter? I was making a break for freedom. As I left the house, a small part of me felt guilty. I might be making it hard for Rion to be a soap bubble again and go back to his mothership or mothercloud or whatever. I might never see him again. Or hear him.

That part cheered me up. And surely something that had lived for over four thousand years was smart enough to figure things out and get back to where it belonged. I was worrying over nothing.

Swinging my bag over my shoulder, I moved quickly down the street.

Chapter Six

It was chilly outside, and I really could have used that jumper Rion had kept nagging me about. Hugging myself, I started to power walk. My house was closer than Jas's so I decided to head there. I'd text Jas and let her know I'd be going home tonight. I didn't think she'd mind much. As for my parents, they'd probably be in bed by now. Luckily I had my house key in my bag. By morning I'd figure out an explanation for why I was home and not at Jas's, and by then I'd be free of that annoying alien.

As I walked I began to feel … not so good. Other than three bites of pizza and half a Coke, I hadn't eaten or drunk anything, so it couldn't be that. My head began to throb; I was feeling dizzy and nauseous. Maybe I was coming down with something. My warm, cosy bed at home started to look more inviting. I quickened my pace.

My head started spinning and I felt like I was going to spew any minute. This night totally sucked, and I'd had such high hopes. It was all Rion's fault. I was sure I would've done better without his interference and schemes, which had done zilch to help me. Ever since Rion had come into my life, it had gone south.

Yuck, be still, stomach. And why were the streetlights wavering? Perhaps I needed to sit down. Looking around, I saw a Poinciana tree on the edge of a front lawn. It had a sturdy, knotted trunk that was just right for leaning against. Scanning for any dogs that might be lurking, I went over to the tree and inched to the ground. Then I drew up my knees, and rested my arms and head on them.

Sucking in the cold night air, I tried to calm my stomach and clear my head. *Breathe in, breath out. It's all good. I'm not going to be sick. I am* not *going to be sick.*

For a minute or two it was touch and go, and then gradually the feeling went. I lifted my head. The streetlight across the road was still wavering, so I didn't trust myself to get up yet. What was wrong with me?

I rested my head against the bark of the tree and closed my eyes to think. Maybe it had been a mistake to leave the party without telling anyone. Maybe I acted a teensy bit rashly. I still had a ten- or fifteen-minute walk before I got home, but right now I didn't think I could put one foot in front of the other.

And I was alone. It was late at night and I was alone. Okay, it wasn't exactly crime central here in suburban Brisbane, but still, things happened.

I was fine, absolutely fine. I just needed a short rest and I could get going again. There was absolutely no reason to worry. No reason at all.

I heard the sound of a car and opened my eyes to see headlights coming from around the corner. I froze and closed my eyes again tightly. What good that was going to do, I didn't know. But I suddenly understood those little kids who think you can't see them because they can't see you. Illogical, but I got it now.

As I heard the car come down the street, I tensed and held my breath. Closer and closer ... and then it passed by. My breath came out in a gush of wind as the sound of the car got fainter and fainter. I opened my eyes again to the cold, dark night.

How ridiculous. What a wimp. Man up, I told myself. I could just hear the stern lecture that soap bubble would give me right now, except it wasn't a soap bubble any longer. 'It' was Rion, a real, live, breathing, teenage boy who made every other guy, even Chad Everett, look dull and boring.

Okay, maybe not Chad Everett, although Chad was fast losing his appeal for me now that I knew there was little chance he'd ever show the remotest interest in me. It wasn't as if I hadn't tried. And I supposed, to give him credit, Rion had also made an effort to help me. For a while it had been kind of fun dancing with him, and it had even caused people to notice me. Maybe it wasn't Rion's fault that Chad wasn't one of them.

I wondered what Rion would do when he found out I'd gone. Would he get the hint and dematerialise back to wherever he'd come from? Maybe his feelings would be hurt. I'd noticed that occasionally he got sensitive over the slightest things. I was sorry about that, because I didn't like hurting anyone, not even him. After all, he thought he was helping me with all that advice.

It was just so hard living with that little voice inside me all the time. Seriously, an alien over four thousand years old and a teenage girl didn't have all that much in common. I needed to be free of Rion, but I didn't mean him any harm. After all, now that we were separate beings I was sure that he'd be okay. I wasn't totally convinced by his story that we had to stay close. He was probably exaggerating; he did that a lot.

Nothing bad would happen to him, would it? Surely not, but how did I know? What if he couldn't get back to his people and got stranded here? What if he dematerialised into that bubble again and someone stomped on him or something? What if …

I closed my mind to any other horror thoughts. I hated to admit it, but I was starting to get worried.

I knew what I had to do. I had to go back. Damn. A conscience is a very inconvenient thing at times.

I wasn't as dizzy as before. I was just about to get up and go when I heard another sound. It was someone running. Pushing down a panic attack, I moved around to the other side of the tree. It was probably just a jogger; a keep-fit freak who thought midnight was the perfect time for a run. But just in case, I crouched and hoped the tree would hide me.

As the footsteps got louder, instead of being sick I started to feel much better. My dizziness had gone and my stomach had settled. Maybe fear and worry had driven my sickness away.

Uh-oh. The jogger's footsteps were slowing to a walk, and they were much closer. Not good. Not good at all. I held my breath again and looked around for a fallen branch or something I could use as a weapon. Nothing in sight at all. Just my luck.

The footsteps slowed and stopped.

'Zoe, what the hell do you think you're doing?'

I wasn't sure if I was disappointed or relieved to hear his voice. I rose and came around to the front of the tree again where he was standing, hands on hips and glowering down at me.

'Rion, what are you doing here?'

'Looking for you, obviously. Have you any idea how many streets I've been down searching for you? Explain.' He was breathing hard and the look he gave me could have melted steel, it was so fiery.

I stepped back from him, judging it wise to put some distance between us. 'I was on my way home, but then—'

'Without telling me, without even telling Jas, whose house you're supposed to be sleeping at tonight.' He never gave me the chance to finish telling him I was on my way back there.

'I would've texted her,' I said in self-defence.

'And what about me?' he said. 'What was I supposed to do? Did you even think about that, Zoe?'

I shifted from one foot to the other, a little uncomfortable and not really sure how to answer that one. If I told him the truth and said I'd wanted to get rid of him I was afraid he'd explode before I could explain that I'd changed my mind. I wondered how angry an alien could get. I hadn't counted on this.

As I tried to work out a plausible explanation, the silence stretched. Rion's heavy breathing and angry vibes filled the air. Then he let out an expression that was partly a loud grunt and partly what sounded like a swearword. But if it was a swearword, it was one I'd never heard before, so maybe it was an alien one.

'You wanted to leave me so you'd be free. That's it, isn't it?'

I didn't answer.

'Of all the ungrateful, narrow-minded, selfish and cruel beings I've ever inhabited, you win the prize. Not even Claudius—and he sent the Christians to the lions in the Coliseum—was as insensitive or unkind to me as you. And General Vigo, who was extremely intelligent, valued my advice highly in his campaign against the French. *He* certainly never wanted to get rid of me. I actually tried to help you. I even went against my better instincts to take this form just so you would look good to your peers and that boy. And this is the thanks I get. I had thought better of you, Zoe.'

He turned his back to me and I could see by the set of his shoulders that he was mega-upset.

I cleared my throat. 'Sorry,' I said. 'I guess I acted a bit impulsively. But I've been thinking it over and I was just about to go back to the party when you came.'

'Do you expect me to believe that?'

'Well, it's true. I started to worry about whether you would be okay and so I decided to go back. And as for

69

being cruel, that's a bit harsh, isn't it? I mean, you could go back to your mothership and all.'

'Mother*cloud*,' he snapped. 'How many times do I have to tell you? And no, I could not. I thought I'd explained all that to you. But I forgot I was dealing with a creature of such low intelligence.'

Maybe if he hadn't added that last bit I might have kept my temper. And he'd kept his back to me, which was also kind of insulting.

'Listen to me,' I said, putting my hands on my hips. 'I never asked you to inhabit me. You've invaded my privacy, my life and even my free will at times. It's so not cool. So back off, you over-inflated egomaniac of a soap bubble.'

He whirled around to face me. 'I never wanted you as a host, either. Do you really think you'd be my first choice? A hormonal, self-entitled teenage girl with zero understanding of the superior being she's dealing with?'

We exchanged death glares for a moment.

Then I said, 'But I'm not your host any more. You're real and separate.' At the moment he seemed very real and human, and so much harder to deal with than a soap bubble. 'What's the big deal if we sever the link? The sooner the better.' I crossed my arms.

For a few moments there was heavy, angry breathing from both of us.

'Because that's not how it works,' he said, making a visible effort to calm down. 'Tell me, Zoe, how do you feel right now?'

I was surprised by the question. 'I've been better. This definitely wouldn't rank in the top ten moments of my life.'

He made an impatient movement with his hand. 'Aside from your moods, which at your age are as changeable as the wind, how do you feel physically?'

'Didn't know you cared. Are you going to give me another lecture on health food and clean living? Seems an odd time to do it, but then you're not very good with timing.'

'Just answer the question, Zoe.'

'Don't get snappy with me again. Well, to tell the truth I've been feeling a bit sick. That's why I sat down by this tree. But I feel much better now.'

'Do you know why you felt sick?'

I shrugged. 'I'm still not seeing the relevance here, but whatever. Maybe it was something I ate, or maybe I've caught something.'

'No, it was neither of those things. I felt sick, too, very sick. The longer you were gone the worse I felt. And do you know why?'

'You missed me?' I grinned at him.

'It's so hard having a serious conversation with you,' he said.

Then he brushed the hair from his forehead. It was such a normal thing to do that, for a microsecond, I wished for a microsecond he were a normal guy. If he was normal then maybe I could learn to like him—as a friend, that is, a guy friend who just happened to look hot. It couldn't hurt.

'Focus, Zoe,' he said, 'and listen carefully.'

I breathed deeply and turned my attention back to what he was saying. He seemed to have an uncanny sense of what I was thinking. Not a comfortable idea. I cleared my mind of all thoughts. 'Go on,' I said.

'We both felt sick because of the bond between us. Remember that I said it was like you were on a leash? That's too simplistic. We're connected, and our wellbeing depends on that connection. The further apart we get, the worse we feel. If we got too far apart the bond would break, but …'

Okay, so maybe he wasn't exaggerating about the connection thing. 'But what?' I asked, not sure if I wanted to hear the answer.

'The consequences would be dire. It would not be good for either one of us.'

Nope, didn't like the sound of that at all. 'What would happen?'

This time it was his turn to shrug. 'We would both cease to exist.'

I hadn't expected that answer. I took a moment and then said, 'Why didn't you tell me?'

'I thought it was obvious.'

'Not to me.'

He rolled his eyes.

'So, what do we do now?'

'I have to dematerialise and inhabit you again,' he said. 'That was always the plan.'

Maybe it was the plan for him, but not for me. I didn't like the thought of my soap bubble returning to my body. 'Is there any other way?'

'You don't seriously expect me to stay like this,' he said.

I looked at him, a six-foot teenage hunk who looked like he should be on a magazine cover. 'You could do worse,' I said.

He sighed. 'Is every teenage girl on the planet so easily swayed by the mere physical looks of the opposite sex?'

Jeez, did that question even need an answer?

'I can't stay like this,' he continued. 'It would be entirely impractical. Where would I live? *How* would I live? You do realise I would always have to remain within a radius of 96.378 metres of you or we would both start to feel unwell.'

I could see the implications of what he said. He was right: it was impractical.

'I have to dematerialise,' he said, 'for both our sakes. It won't be so bad. We'll get used to each other and maybe, by the time you're thirty or forty and have matured a little, we might even get to like each other.'

Life with a talking bubble. Forever. But, sadly, the alternative was worse.

'Okay. I guess you have to do it. So go on, get it over with. Should I close my eyes again?'

'That's probably best.' He put his hands on my arms. 'Zoe, I know this is hard for you, so thank you.' He bent towards me and kissed my forehead.

I nearly teared up then. I took one last look at this beautiful alien and said, 'Goodbye, Rion.' I closed my eyes. 'Let's get on with it, then.'

Chapter Seven

I thought I would feel something when he dematerialised, but I didn't feel anything except depressed. It was one thing to know Rion, the not-so-bad-looking boy, who, although he had an ego problem and spoke way too much, seemed so real. It was something else entirely to have him right there inside my head—usually telling me what to do. That? Not so good. Still, it seemed the only solution.

I waited for a while, and when I didn't feel or hear anything I opened my eyes. Rion was still beside me. His eyes were closed and his face was like a death mask, all calm and still.

'You're still here,' I said, stating the obvious.

'I know. I'm concentrating. Shh.'

I waited and watched. He breathed deeply and stretched out his hands to touch my shoulders. I could feel the touch of his fingers and the warmth of his breath on my forehead. It was so hard to believe he was going to disappear in a few moments.

But he didn't.

After what seemed ages he dropped his hands and opened his eyes. 'It isn't working,' he said, a puzzled frown wrinkling his brow. 'I don't know what's wrong.'

'You've done this before, right?'

'Only once before, and I only took human form for a few minutes. I've been in this body now for three hours, thirteen minutes and ... forty-two, no, forty-three seconds. Perhaps that's the problem.' He was looking really worried now. 'I've been an organic for too long.'

'Maybe it's something else. Try and remember exactly what you did last time,' I said, trying to be reassuring.

Rion put his hands on his waist and closed his eyes again. A look of intense concentration came over his face. After a few minutes his breath came out in a gush, as if he'd been holding it, and he opened his eyes.

'I can't do it,' he said, shaking his head. 'I just can't do it. I can't revert to my original state.'

I could see he was completely devastated. 'Maybe you're tired or something,' I said. 'You might have to wait until you're rested and have all your powers again.'

He shook his head. Moving to the tree, he sank down to the ground and dropped his head into his hands. I wasn't used to seeing him like this. In the time I'd known him he'd been a smartarse know-it-all who had never doubted his abilities.

I sat down beside him. 'Just give it time. I'm sure it'll work.'

He raised his head and there was moisture in his eyes. 'Don't you understand? I've lost who I was. I gave up my superior form to become a lesser creature, and I did it just to pander to my pride. You set me a challenge and I couldn't help taking it up. And then I started to show off, basking in the praise of adolescent teenagers as if I was merely a couple of thousand years old instead of the experienced and mature being I've become in over four millennia. And for that, I've been punished. I heard stories of this happening to one or two of my kind. I thought they were merely legends told to the young as cautionary tales against becoming too involved with our hosts. Now I see that they were true. Now I know it's dangerous to stay in a physical form for any length of time.'

'That sucks,' I said, trying to be sympathetic.

'That sucks,' he mimicked, giving me a withering look. 'What a master of understatement that is. It doesn't just suck; it's a catastrophic situation of tragically epic proportions.

Here I am, a highly intelligent being, a shining example of my race, forced to exist as a creature that would barely measure on any scale of knowledge or understanding. Your race has hardly made any progress since the first caveman scratched a drawing on a cave wall.'

My sympathy was fast disappearing.

'I don't know what to do,' he said.

'Maybe you should've taken more notice of those legends,' I said. 'Obviously someone of my limited understanding can't help you here.'

'Yes, so true.'

He still didn't get sarcasm.

Just then my phone buzzed. Pulling it out of my pocket, I saw it was Jas. Oops, I'd forgotten to text her.

Where are you?

I thought for a moment and replied: *Got tired and decided to go home. Soz, forgot to text you.*

You should have said. How did you get home?

Walked.

At this time of night!! Are you crazy?

I looked over at my alien. *It's okay. Rion came with me.*

Oh. Is he staying at yours?

A pointed although good question. If Rion couldn't turn back into a soap bubble, where would he stay? I sent a reply: *No, but nearby. Gotta go. See you Monday.*

Yeah. We need to talk soon.

Jas was not happy, and it was clear she wanted explanations about why her nerdy friend left early and managed to take the hottest boy at the party—aside from Chad Everett—with her. I was starting to realise all the problems Rion would cause if he stayed around.

Slipping my phone back into my pocket, I said, 'Okay, what now?'

Rion looked at me, his eyes filled with misery. 'What do you mean? My life is effectively over.'

'Well, mine isn't. So get your smart arse into gear and start working out a solution to our problem with your supposedly superior brain. That is, if it's still functioning.'

Tough love, perhaps, but we needed to do something soon. Well, tough anyway, but definitely no love. I was seriously annoyed with this alien. We couldn't sit against this tree all night.

It seemed to work. He straightened up and pushed the hair from his forehead.

'Obviously I need a place to stay,' he said, 'and the means to keep this body properly nourished and maintained. Perhaps your parents would let me stay in the spare room. I would certainly be a useful houseguest. I could help your mother with healthy recipes and useful cooking tips, and give her advice about those infants she teaches. Your father could certainly use my business acumen in his job, and of course I'd be invaluable to you with your homework, that is, if you could be bothered to listen to me. You usually don't. But anyway, that would prove an acceptable temporary solution until I can find somewhere better.'

'Hold on a minute. You're getting ahead of yourself, buddy. What am I supposed to tell my parents about you? I can't just turn up with some stray guy I want them to look after. You're making a whole lot of assumptions here.'

'Why, we'll tell them the truth, of course. I'm sure when they understand the situation they'll be most accommodating.'

I looked at him in disbelief. 'You're joking, right?'

'I fail to see the humour in that.'

'My parents will think you're mad.'

'You mean they won't believe me?'

'Got it in one. They'll probably call the police, or children's services.'

'I am *not* a child,' Rion said, looking insulted.

'No, but you are a minor, which means being under eighteen.'

'I'm over four thousand Earth years old,' he said.

'Well, you look sixteen or seventeen, and that's what they'll think you are. If you haven't got a home and sound a bit loopy they might decide to check you out. If you're lucky, you might get a nice foster family.' I hoped I was making my point. For someone who thought he was smart, he sure didn't get a lot of things. 'Or maybe they'll find a nice mental asylum for you,' I added.

'Perhaps I should think of a better strategy.'

'Yeah, and while you're thinking, let's start moving. I need to get home.'

I went to stand up, but Rion rose quickly and reached out a hand to pull me up. I felt stiff and sore after sitting so long, and I suddenly realised how cold I was. I shivered.

He put one arm around me and pulled me close. 'Body heat is a very effective way of maintaining core temperature,' he said.

I knew it didn't mean anything, but I had to admit it was very nice snuggling into Rion. I leaned my head against his shoulder and our feet started moving. In some ways Rion the boy was far superior to a bubble.

For a while neither of us said anything, which was a first, but as we got closer to home I started to worry about what to do with him. Rion might have been a genius when it came to maths. He might have knowledge of history that rivalled the information in the State Library. He might even have been able to recite the entire works of Shakespeare, something I actively discouraged after he tried to quote *Hamlet* from start to finish one night. But he seemed to have absolutely zero understanding of the real world and how it worked.

I couldn't tell Mum and Dad about him, that was a certainty, at least not until I'd worked out some plausible explanation. And that could take time. Until then I had to figure out where he could stay.

When we reached my house he dropped his arm. I immediately felt cold again. I couldn't wait to be in my own bed and for this night to be over.

'I guess I'll have to stay in your room tonight and talk to your parents in the morning,' he said.

'Are you nuts? What do you think Mum and Dad would say to that?'

He looked at me in puzzlement. 'But, Zoe, I've been with you for three weeks now. It's never been a problem before, although I hate to mention that you do snore. That's been quite disconcerting at times.'

'I. Do. Not. Jeez, one thing about you hasn't changed. You're still mega-annoying, and totally clueless about real life. You're not some irritating little voice inside me now, you know. You're a person, and a guy. That makes all the difference. Surely even you can see that.'

I saw a look of understanding cross his face. 'Oh, I see. It wouldn't be appropriate. I sometimes forget those tiresome little customs and rules you have. They've never applied to me before. It's so inconvenient being human.' He sighed and crossed his arms, looking like a poster for some teen flick or TV show. If only he was a bit more ugly, it would be so easy to dislike him.

'Yes, not appropriate at all,' I said. 'But I think I have a solution, a temporary one, at least.'

I'd been looking in the direction of the shed in our yard, where we kept our boat. It needed some repairs, so Dad wouldn't be using it any time soon. I took Rion's hand and dragged him across the lawn.

'You can stay in here for now and in the morning we'll figure something out.' I surprised myself with my own brilliance at times.

'In that hut?' he said. 'It looks rather uncomfortable.'

'Better than sleeping under a tree,' I said unsympathetically. What did he want, five-star accommodation?

I went to the side door of the shed and reached up to the ledge for the key. As I opened the door it gave a squeak that seemed to echo in the night air. I looked around and held my breath, hoping I hadn't wakened Mum or Dad. After a few moments, when nothing happened, I gave a sigh of relief. Stepping inside, I flicked on the light, pulled Rion in and closed the door behind us.

The boat was a small cabin cruiser with a minuscule space inside that held a couple bunks. The boat was hardly big enough for the three of us when we went out, and we'd only slept on board once or twice, but at least it would do for now. I just had to hope Dad didn't want to clean the boat or anything.

'Come on, climb up,' I said to Rion.

After we'd clambered aboard, I showed him the bunks in the cabin below. He was less than impressed.

'There's no bedding, and I can hardly stand up in here. I'll probably get extremely cold and hardly sleep.'

I reached under one of the bunks and pulled out a drawer. Mum had taken all the blankets to wash them, so I grabbed an old picnic rug and shoved it in his arms. 'Welcome to the real world,' I said.

Chapter Eight

I was dead tired when I finally got into bed, but for once I didn't have that little bubble inside me giving a lecture on the benefits of a good night's sleep and the joy of a jog around the block at six in the morning. I could eat what I wanted for breakfast and not be given a breakdown on the nutritional value of muesli as opposed to Coco Pops. I wouldn't even have to endure a nagging session about doing homework on Sunday morning rather than leaving it until half an hour before class the next day.

It was a wonderful, liberating feeling. At least it should have been. But I was worried.

What was I going to do with a 4000-year-old alien who was inhabiting the body of a sixteen-year-old boy, and who was so connected to me that we couldn't be more than a hundred metres apart without dire consequences? How was I going to explain him to my parents, to my friends, and to anyone else who happened to come across him? Rion might look like a teenage guy, but he sure didn't act or sound or like one.

Life sucked at the moment.

And so, despite feeling like I could've gone to sleep standing up, I didn't sleep a wink—until dawn, and then I crashed.

It wasn't until I heard the distant sound of a lawnmower that my eyes slowly opened to a room full of sunshine. For a moment I was tempted to roll over and go back to sleep. After all, it was Sunday and I'd gone to a party last night.

Sunday.

Party.

Rion.

Oh my God.

I bolted upright and grabbed my phone. It was eleven am and I was still in bed. What was happening with Rion? Had anyone discovered him yet? And why hadn't I set an alarm?

Bouncing out of bed, I pulled on my jeans and grabbed a clean T-shirt from my drawer. Then I shoved my feet into thongs and headed for the kitchen, which, thankfully, was empty. I saw a note propped up against the microwave.

Hi darling, Dad and I just out at the markets if you get home before we do. Hope you had a nice time at Jas's. See you soon. xx Mum

I closed my eyes and thanked all the gods in this world and the next for such luck. My parents hadn't realised I'd come home last night. Not only would I not have to come up with an explanation for why I'd slept in my own bed and not at Jas's, but I also had time to get Rion out of the boat.

I raced out to the backyard and went into the shed.

'Rion,' I called in a loud whisper. I didn't want any nosy neighbours wondering what was happening.

No answer.

I climbed onto the boat, thinking he was still probably sleeping. Bending down and looking into the small cabin, my heart did a flip-flop. The plaid picnic blanket was neatly folded at the foot of one of the bunks but there was no one there. Rion was missing.

My first instinct was to panic. Then I remembered the distance thing between us. I felt okay, so I knew he couldn't be that far away. Maybe he'd gone for a walk or something—a short one.

I climbed out of the boat and looked around. I saw Mr Gallagher across the street pushing his mower. I gave him a wave and hoped Rion hadn't talked to him or anything. There was no guarantee Rion wouldn't say something entirely stupid.

Why couldn't he have stayed put? It was like losing a puppy; you just knew the pup would get into trouble.

I walked down the street, hoping I would see him. But I started to feel sick, so I realised I wasn't heading in the right direction. I turned back and headed in the other direction. Same thing happened. I knew he had to be somewhere close by, so I returned to our house. I had to find him before my parents returned.

Searching the backyard with no result, I went into the house again. And there he was, sitting at the kitchen table eating a bowl of muesli and with a glass of water in front of him.

'Good morning, Zoe,' he said, and flashed me a smile as if it was the most normal thing in the world for him to be there. He was looking clean and fresh, even though he still had on the same dark T-shirt and jeans from yesterday.

'Where were you? I looked everywhere.' I collapsed in the chair opposite him.

'I needed to use your bathroom, and then I decided that while I was there I might as well use your shower. I hope you don't mind.' He took a spoonful of muesli and chewed it thoughtfully.

I'd obviously been in such a hurry when I got up that I hadn't noticed anyone was in my bathroom.

'But what about my parents?' I said. 'Please tell me they didn't see you.'

He put down his spoon. 'No, of course not,' he said. 'I heard them leave this morning and saw their note when I came into the house, so I knew I'd have time to refresh myself and have some nourishment before they returned.' He took another spoon of cereal and winced. 'This isn't quite as delicious as I'd imagined. However, I'm sure its nutritional benefits outweigh its taste.'

I let out the breath I'd been holding and resisted the urge to shake him. 'Okay, just hurry up. It's nearly noon and that's when the markets finish. They could be home any minute. We've got to get you out of here and think of a strategy.'

'Well, you could always say I was a boy you met at the party and I came over to see you,' he said calmly. 'That would be within the realms of possibility, wouldn't it?'

'You mean like a boyfriend or something?'

He shrugged. 'Whatever.'

I looked at him in surprise. 'Pardon? What did you say?'

'I said "whatever". Isn't that what you say sometimes?'

'Yeah, but you don't talk like me, or like any normal teenager I know.'

'No, but it did occur to me that perhaps I need to adopt the verbal patterns of a twenty-first-century adolescent if I want to avoid suspicion.'

'Jeez, you've still got a long way to go. Aren't you finished that muesli yet?'

He sighed and shoved the bowl away. 'Yes. Somehow it just isn't satisfying me at the moment. Do you wish to go for a walk so we can formulate a plan?'

I grabbed the bowl and put it in the sink. 'Yes, you got it. And I hope you have some good ideas floating around in that oversized brain of yours. And I can't say I met you at the party because they don't know I went to one. Never mind. We'll think of something.'

'So,' I said, as we sauntered down the street, 'how long are you going to stay like this? Could you contact someone in your race and let them know what's happened? Surely your *superior* race can come up with a solution.' I couldn't help adding that last bit.

'Yes, someone will contact me shortly. It's difficult for me to communicate with my people directly, although I'll try. Once we have a human host, we believe we need to completely immerse ourselves in that life span in order to fully comprehend your species. Normally we would only be contacted directly by our people if there was some sort of crisis, which obviously this is.'

'But that's good,' I said with relief. Maybe there would be a quick way out of this after all. 'So, within the next day or two?'

Rion looked at me as if I had two heads or something. 'Of course not,' he said. 'Our concept of time is quite different from that of your short-lived species. If I'm lucky, someone in the upper echelons will be in touch within the next ten to fifteen years, quite soon actually.'

I stopped mid-stride and stared at him. 'Ten to fifteen years! I can't be stuck with you for that long.'

Rion lifted a perfect eyebrow. 'On the contrary, it's I who will be stuck with you. Not my ideal scenario. However, if I thought it was only a decade or so I could put up with it.'

'*You* might. *I* couldn't. Isn't there anything you can do to hurry it along a bit?'

'They probably won't even notice what's happened to me for a year or two.'

'Kill me now.'

Rion sighed heavily. 'You do have the most histrionic expressions. Look on the bright side. If I'd stayed in my original state as a superior consciousness inside you—assuming a physical, human form is something I will never do again—we would be bonded for the remainder of your life. Although considering your diet, that could well be of short duration.'

He gave a little shrug as if it were completely irrelevant to him, and then added, 'This way we might be free of each other by the time you're thirty, if we're lucky. I think I could put up with the situation for that long. After all, I imagine it would be similar to having a pet, like a dog.'

'You know what? You may look hot, but you are, without a doubt, the most mega-annoying, seriously unlikeable, totally uncool guy I have ever known, and that's saying something.'

I was over this. I had a good mind to walk away from Rion right then and there, and too bad about the being sick and everything. It had been bad enough when I could only hear him, but now I could see *and* hear him. And I had to look after him and make sure he didn't get into trouble until I was maybe *thirty*. If he'd been halfway likeable perhaps it wouldn't be so bad. But he had zero personality, and zero feelings for anyone but himself.

Maybe I was just tired, but suddenly I couldn't handle this anymore. I turned away from him to hide the tears forming in my eyes. The last thing I wanted was to show him any weakness. It would only be something else he could feel superior about. For a moment I couldn't speak because if I did I might say or do something stupid.

'You wish to turn back, Zoe? Zoe?'

I felt a sob welling up and I pushed it down.

'You're upset,' he said.

Still couldn't talk.

'Have I upset you?'

Jeez, I thought, this alien was supposed to be smart.

I felt his hand on my arm and he turned me around to face him. He looked puzzled. 'You're about to cry. What have I done or said?'

'What the hell do you think, alien? You insult me with every second word. You think I'm stupid, that I'm not going to live long, and you never stop for one moment to consider anyone else's feelings but your own. That is, assuming you have any. Have you ever stopped to think what you're doing to me, how you've completely ruined my life? Honestly, Rion, you're a complete jerk.'

I was surprised I got all those words out. But then I knew my eyes were going to start leaking water like a dripping tap so I spun on my heel and headed away from him, fast. I hadn't got very far when he caught up with me.

'Zoe, wait.'

He darted in front of me and I collided with his chest. His arms went around me automatically, and the dam inside me burst. For a few moments I made a complete embarrassing fool of myself. But I couldn't help it. For once, Rion didn't say anything but just held me in an awkward hug. Even though I really wanted to hate him—and almost did—it was hard not to feel some comfort against his broad, warm chest and in the strong arms that were holding me.

I started to calm down and finally my sobs became a few hiccups. Then they stopped and I tried to compose myself.

As my breathing calmed I became conscious of the beating of his heart; how strange that something like that could make me feel better. It almost made me forget that Rion wasn't human. But I didn't *want* to forget.

I moved away from him and looked around the empty street, hoping no one had seen me. 'Sorry, didn't mean to break down like that,' I mumbled.

'No, I've been at fault, Zoe.' He put a finger under my chin and tilted it up so I could see what almost looked like concern in his face. 'I'm not used to having a human form. It's … disconcerting. I've made mistakes. I didn't mean to upset you. In fact, I was trying to comfort you. Perhaps I expressed myself badly. It occurs to me that perhaps I don't understand your species as well as I thought. I'll need help, and maybe, if you feel you can, you'll show me what I need to know.'

Our eyes met, and for the first time since I'd known him we made a connection, one that was real and not just an inconvenience.

'I'm sorry,' he said. 'Please forgive me.'

'Okay, I guess,' I said.

He flashed me his million-dollar smile. 'Good. And,' he added, 'you're far superior to a dog.'

Was that actually an attempt at humour, or did he honestly think he was giving me a compliment? It was hard to know.

I took a deep breath. I was so not ready for this, but it didn't matter. Somehow we had to find a way to explain Rion to my parents, work out where and how he would live, and, last but not least, stay within a hundred metres of each other for the next ten or fifteen years.

Piece of cake, really.

Chapter Nine

Hey, Mum and Dad, this is Rion, a friend of mine. Can he sleep in the spare room, go to school with me and stay until I graduate? Oh, he'll probably go to university with me as well. By the way, he hasn't got any family, at least not in this world, and no money either.'

Rion and I were sitting on the swings in the park near my house. I turned to him and said, 'Yeah, that'll go down well.'

'Don't forget I'll have to stay within a hundred metres of you, and that includes going on all your dates with the opposite sex, and of course when you eventually get married I'll have to live with you and your husband.'

I looked at him, speechless with dismay.

He laughed. It was a deep, husky laugh, and if I hadn't felt so miserable it might have made me laugh, too. As it was, I really didn't see that this was a laughing matter.

And then he said, 'You know, I think I finally understand your sense of humour.'

'That wasn't funny.'

'I beg to differ. I found your reaction most diverting.'

'Well, it wasn't helpful and I really need help here. What am I going to say to Mum and Dad?'

He considered for a moment. 'You could say I'm from out of town and my parents are divorced. After all, that's the story you told at the party. But, of course, we won't mention that detail. We'll say my father's left the country. He's gone to England or somewhere, which is conveniently far away. My mother and I had a disagreement so she asked me to leave. I need a place to live, and since you're my friend you've asked me to stay.'

'Your mum kicked you out? Why?'

'She's taken on a new partner who doesn't like me.'

I bit my tongue on that one. There was no point adding that it wasn't surprising. 'Okay, but my mum will insist on contacting her. And how did you become such a good friend? I've never even mentioned you before. Lot of loopholes in that story.'

He thought for a moment. 'Then my mother sent me to live with my uncle, who didn't realise I was coming and is also out of town, but because I didn't want to stay by myself you said I could stay with you. You met me when you were on holiday at the beach recently and we later became friends—'

'On Facebook,' I said. 'And because your uncle lives nearby, you decided to drop in on me.'

'Yes, that'll do. I've heard of Facebook, although my previous host wasn't very technologically proficient. He was eighty-seven when he died.'

'Don't want to know about that,' I said. It felt creepy to know my alien had inhabited other humans. 'My mum will still want to contact someone from your family to check if it's all right that you stay with us.'

'She's very conscientious, isn't she?'

'That's one way of putting it,' I said.

Over-protective, over-anxious and as square as they come, was another. Even Dad said that Mum had never broken a rule in her life. But I had to admit she was also kind, generous and loving. A homeless teenage boy was sure to appeal to her mothering instincts, providing we could come up with a convincing story.

'My mother lost her phone so she can't be contacted,' Rion said.

'Then how did she get in touch with your uncle?'

'She wrote him a letter, but he mustn't have received it before he went away. He likes to travel to distant places so he's not easy to get in touch with.' Rion gave me a smug look, obviously feeling pleased with himself.

I looked at him. 'I don't know. That story has more holes than Jade Buchanan's crochet top, under which, by the way, she wears a black bra. And my parents go on about what *I* wear. Go figure. Anyway, back to the point. A letter is lame. No one writes letters any more.'

He shrugged. 'She lost her phone, remember.'

'Don't you have one?'

'Theoretically I'm sixteen years old. Why would I have a phone?'

'Boy, do you have a lot to learn. We'll just say you broke it or something, and your mum can't afford to get you another.'

'I'm poor, then?'

'Apparently, because you have no place to stay and no money, buddy. We'll say that when you got to your uncle's place a neighbour told you he's gone to the Brazilian rainforest for three months. He could be a photographer or journalist or something.'

'I thought you said we were poor.'

'You and your mum are, but not her brother and he's sooo tired of bailing her out. The last thing he needs is his nephew staying with him. But he would let you stay if he was here. As a matter of fact, you know you could stay there but it would be lonely. Your mum and her partner have already gone to Cairns to live and there's no way you wanted to go with them.'

'How can she afford to go to Cairns?'

'Her partner's footing the bill, but not for you. And besides, Cairns isn't that far away. Jeez, cut me some slack here. I'm giving your flimsy story a little credibility.'

'Thank you, Zoe, I believe we're ready to approach your parents now.'

'I guess. You haven't got any stuff with you, but we'll say you left it at your uncle's place. Just one more thing,' I said. 'Please try to talk like a normal person and not a walking dictionary.'

He nodded. 'I will endeavour to do my best.'

I looked at him.

'Sure,' he said, 'will do.'

'So you're on your own now, with no one to look after you?' My mum's brown eyes filled with sympathy. 'You poor boy.'

'Isn't there any way of contacting your mother to let her know about the situation?' My father's tone was disapproving.

Rion shook his head. I could see that he was trying to look sad and dejected. 'No, sir,' he said. 'After she lost her phone, her partner Alf said she had to wait until she got a job in Cairns to get another. She said she'd write when she was settled.'

'Doesn't Alf have a phone?' Dad asked.

'I don't have his number and my phone's broken. We didn't exactly part on good terms.' More sad looks; I had to admit Rion was playing his part well.

'So you can't contact your uncle either.' My dad was nothing if not persistent.

'Jeez, Dad, he's in the Brazilian rainforest,' I said, hoping the questions were coming to an end.

But my mum came to the rescue. She laid her hand on my dad's arm. 'I think that's enough questions for now. Of course you can stay, Rion. Zoe, show him upstairs to the guest room.'

I closed the door as soon as we got upstairs and sank onto the bed, exhausted.

Rion sat in the corner armchair. He folded his hands in his lap and gave me a calm look. 'That went smoothly, didn't it?'

For someone who was supposed to be so smart, he sure didn't read people very well.

'No,' I said, 'we barely scraped by with that story. My mum overlooked the small details because she's worried about you, but she'll get to them eventually. Dad was super-suspicious. Just keep a low profile for today. We'll go to the mall or something. We need to get out of here before they ask any more questions.'

He nodded. 'Yes, that'll give us some thinking time.'

I looked at him through narrowed eyes. 'For someone who's always going on about honesty you sure have adapted quickly to a life of deception.'

'I'm a fast learner. And you've been an excellent teacher.' He gave me a cheeky smile.

At the mall Rion was totally rapt by everything. You'd think he'd never been here a dozen times with me before when he was that annoying little bubble inside me.

'What a rainbow of colours and a cacophony of sound.' He looked around the very ordinary foodcourt. 'And there's a veritable feast of aromas.'

'Excuse me, is that English you're speaking? Remember, you're sixteen right now, not a 4000-plus-years-old alien.'

'Cocker spaniel.'

'What?'

'I'll have to remember to have a vocabulary that's slightly more advanced than an average cocker spaniel would understand.'

'Gee, thanks for that,' I said. 'You do realise dogs don't talk.'

'That's true, but they do understand a limited number of words.' He looked at me and seemed to realise he'd said something insulting. 'Oh, sorry, perhaps I should've phrased that differently.'

'Ya think? Anyway, what's the big deal about the shopping centre? You've been here heaps of times.'

He sniffed the air appreciatively. 'But everything I experienced was only secondhand, through you. I've never actually smelled or tasted anything for myself before. It's overwhelming. What is that divine aroma?'

I looked over in the direction he was staring.' McDonald's,' I said with a touch of smugness, thinking of the trillions of lectures from him on the evils of junk food.

'Surely not,' he said, turning a devastated face to me.

'Are you hungry?'

He stopped to think about it for a moment. 'You know,' he said, 'I believe I am. There is a certain emptiness in my stomach.'

'You want a Big Mac? I brought money.'

For a moment he wavered, but then he said, 'No, I think I'd better choose a healthier alternative. Perhaps some carrots, or a salad or green tea.'

I sighed. 'No one is ever going to believe that you're a teenager. Come on, there's a salad bar over there, though it's a waste of seven dollars fifty, if you ask me.'

A few minutes later we were seated at a table, me with my cheeseburger and fries, and Rion with his salad and tea. He pushed the dark fringe off his forehead and picked up his fork. He put a mouthful of greens in his mouth and chewed carefully.

'Hmm,' he said, 'most refreshing.'

I took a bite of cheeseburger and washed it down with a sip of Coke. 'If you say so.'

'And there are so many vitamins and minerals in this, not to mention the antioxidants in the green tea.'

'You'll be the healthiest teen in Brisbane,' I said, popping a fry in my mouth.

We ate in silence for a few minutes. Rion chewed each mouthful slowly, and when he was finished he put down his fork. He wiped his mouth carefully with the napkin and took a sip of tea.

'Ouch, it's hot,' he said, quickly putting the cup down.

'Of course, it's tea.'

'I didn't think it would be so hot.'

I pushed my Coke over to him. 'Here, take a sip of that. It's cold.'

'Thank you, it might sooth the burning sensation.' He took the cup and drank from it. 'Oh, that's much better.'

'Tastes better too, doesn't it?' I quirked an eyebrow at him.

'No, of course not, it's laden with chemicals and sugar,' he said, but he took another sip.

'You know, I really can't finish these fries. Would you like one?'

'No, thank you, I'm perfectly satisfied with this salad.'

I shrugged. 'Suit yourself.'

He hesitated. 'Well, maybe just one, in the interests of curiosity and scientific observation.' He took a chip and bit it carefully. 'It actually tastes ... not bad.'

'Here, try it with barbecue sauce.' I pushed the little sachet towards him.

He took another chip and dipped it in. He closed his eyes and licked his lips. Okay, that kind of distracted me. It was so unfair of the universe to put my alien into a seriously hot body. The personality does not match the bod, I told myself. Remember that, Zoe. *Focus. Focus.*

He opened his eyes. 'Quite interesting. I'm beginning to understand the addiction of fast food. But it really isn't good for you, Zoe. The high fat content of those chips alone would seriously raise your cholesterol levels if you ate them on a regular basis.'

How quickly that hunk factor vanished when he opened his mouth and words came out.

'Yeah, yeah, whatever,' I said. 'You ready to go?'

'Where?'

'We have to buy you some stuff. You can't survive in one pair of jeans and a T-shirt for the next ten years.'

I had some savings that I'd hoped to use on a GHD hair straightener and maybe some new jeans, but at the moment Rion's needs were greater than mine. For now I'd have to put up with wavy hair and last year's jeans.

He looked down at his clothes with a frown. 'I suppose you're right. I manifested these garments when I materialised, but I can only do it once. I will need more clothing, but first I'll need some currency. And I'll have to get employment of some kind. There really are some complications to being in a human body. One has so many needs.'

'First things first,' I said. 'You haven't even got a toothbrush. And don't worry about money for now. I've got some.' I stood up and grabbed his hand. 'Come on. Let's go shopping.'

Chapter Ten

Shopping. Usually that's a word that makes me feel happy. And naturally it takes time. I mean, who buys the first thing they try on? Half the fun is trying on loads of things and then deciding what makes you look the best, and also finding something you can actually afford, or nearly afford, as long as you don't go anywhere, or buy anything for the next month.

I had a small source of income. I babysat occasionally for family friends and friends of friends. It wasn't going to buy me the latest iPhone or Nikes, although I did have a pretty good fake pair, but it kept me from dire poverty.

Mum and Dad wouldn't let me work at any of the fast-food outlets where some of my friends had part-time jobs. They had this old-fashioned idea that school was more important and that I needed good grades so I could get into university. I wasn't a nerd or anything—God forbid—and I wasn't totally against getting an education, but jeez, priorities here. I didn't really mind not having a part-time job, but I sure wasn't going to stop having a social life, no matter what they said.

Anyway, shopping equalled good vibes. Usually. But shopping with Rion was another scene altogether.

I guided Rion through the doors of Target. I knew it would all have to be budget stuff, but luckily for us the sales were on. If there was one thing I loved, it was a sale.

'Right,' I said, 'you need several tops, a jumper, undies and a toothbrush.'

In the men's section Rion picked up a check shirt with a button-down collar that was at least three sizes too big for him.

'This'll do,' he said.

'Yeah, sure, if you were about fifty years old and weighed a hundred kilos. Besides, you have to try stuff on first.' I took the shirt from him and put it back.

'Try it on? That seems unnecessary, and very time consuming.'

'Jeez, Rion, how else are you going to know if it fits or looks good on you?'

'That shirt would've covered me, and since clothes are purely functional what it looks like is irrelevant.' He picked up another shirt. It was Hawaiian with large pink flowers and palm ferns. 'How about this?' he said.

'Are you serious? Do you actually want to be the laughingstock of everyone, not to mention being a prime target for bullying?'

He put it down, reluctantly. 'It's very colourful,' he said.

'My point exactly.'

I scanned the racks for something he could actually wear, then grabbed a couple of dark T-shirts and a pair of jeans that were on special. Holding the shirts up to him, I gave a critical assessment as to size. 'These should do. Now go try them on.'

'All this?' he said. 'I don't need this much.'

'Yes, you do.' I grabbed his hand, dragged him over to the dressing room and gave him a push. 'Go in there, put them on, and then come out and show me.'

I sat down in the chair just outside the cubicle. There was no way I was going to trust Rion's judgement on what fit or looked good.

'Did you know, Zoe, that you have a very domineering side to your personality?'

'Do you want to fit in or not? If you don't look normal, people are going to think there's something weird about you and start asking questions. I mean, you already sound different. You don't want to look different, too.'

He sighed. 'I suppose you have a point.' He disappeared into the dressing room.

A few minutes later he came out wearing the T-shirt back to front and the jean legs folded up like he was going line dancing or something. All he needed to complete the image was a pair of cowboy boots.

'I thought it would be cooler that way and give my body more ventilation,' was his explanation.

This was going to be a long afternoon.

Finally, after forcing him to try on a heap more clothes, we had a couple of T-shirts, one long-sleeved shirt, jeans and a black jumper that was half price. Rion had protested about almost everything we bought. It seemed he didn't want me to spend so much money. Who knew that an alien could be so worried over stuff like that?

Now there was only the matter of some socks and undies. I thought I could probably leave that with him. I really didn't feel like going through the underwear section with him. And after all, even Rion couldn't go wrong with socks and jocks.

I gave him some money. 'You need to buy some underwear and socks,' I said. 'I'll meet you in that coffee place outside. I seriously need some caffeine.' He looked ready to complain again, but I cut him off. 'It's a question of hygiene.' Then I went into a few details about how to pay. I crossed my fingers. Surely nothing could go wrong.

He nodded and I escaped outside. I started to feel a bit queasy, so I knew Rion must be further than a hundred metres from me. I hadn't realised the shop was so big or that the men's section was so far away from the coffee shop. I was just beginning to go through all the inconveniences that would become part of my life from now on when Rion came out carrying a bag and looking pleased with himself.

I nearly choked on my latte.

He was wearing the jeans and he'd rolled them up again, despite my telling him that it was so not cool, in a fashion sense, that is. But that wasn't the worst part. He was wearing fluorescent pink socks that could only have come from the women's section. I didn't even want to think about the underwear he'd bought.

'What do you think?' he asked, hitching up his jeans so I could see even more of those hideous socks.

I grabbed his hands so he had to let go of his jeans and pulled him down onto the chair beside me. 'Are you serious?' I hissed.

He looked at me, all perplexed and innocent. 'What? I thought you'd be pleased. I even tried them on first.'

I was glad I hadn't been there to see that. Did he have to take things so literally?

'Look around, Rion. Look at the guys your age, actually at any guys at all. Do you see any of them wearing pink socks?'

He scanned the crowded mall and then looked back at me. 'No, I guess not. Male clothing isn't very colourful, is it? Perhaps I should have materialised as a female. It would've been more convenient in many ways. We could've shared garments. It certainly would have been cheaper.'

I closed my eyes and counted to ten. Patience was not my strong point, and at the moment it was being stretched to its outer limits. I opened them again. 'That would've defeated the whole purpose of you materialising in the first place, wouldn't it?' I was trying very hard not to be sarcastic.

'Of course,' he said, 'how remiss of me not to remember. It was to make that boy jealous. By the way, I hope you're still not attracted.'

'No, Chad made it clear he only has eyes for Jas.'

'I don't mean Chad. It was plain that the two of you are not suited.'

'Then who are you talking about?'

'Me, of course,' he said. 'From your elevated temperature and pulse rate when we were dancing, I deduced that you were highly attracted to me.'

I pierced him with a look. 'And what are your deductions right at this moment, smarty pants?'

He moved away from me slightly. 'I think that is probably no longer the case.'

'You're not even close. I was never, ever attracted to you, you soap bubble in a mannequin's body. And every time you speak there's less chance I ever will be. End of conversation.' I picked up my coffee cup and took a calming sip.

He folded his arms and put on a broody look that some might even call sulky. I ignored him.

'Hey, Zoe ... and Rion.'

The surprise was evident in Jas's voice as she came up to us. She was laden with bags. I might have liked shopping, but Jas lived for it. And with well-off parents who were generous, it was something she did a lot. But why did she have to turn up right now?

Without an invitation—Jas believed she was welcome anywhere and in most cases she was right—she sat down at our table and plunked her bags next to her feet.

'What are you guys doing here? I thought you'd be heading home by now, Rion. You said you were only here for the weekend, didn't you?'

'There's been a change of plan,' he said. 'I'm staying with Zoe and her parents for a while.'

'What?'

I totally enjoyed Jas's look of astonishment. Her thoughts were as plain as if they'd been written in a speech bubble above her head. *Hot guy staying with Zoe, impossible!*

'Yes, I was going to stay with my uncle, but he's away at the moment and Zoe's parents kindly offered to let me stay with them.' The lies flowed so smoothly from Rion's mouth.

'Really? So does that mean you're staying for a while?' Her eyes got all glow-y like.

'For the foreseeable future,' he replied.

'Cool. So what about school and everything?'

He hesitated, and with a sinking feeling I knew what the answer would be. 'I'll be going where Zoe goes.'

He looked over at me and I nodded. Having to stay within a hundred metres of each other didn't allow for separate schools or separate anywheres. It was a depressing thought.

'That's fantastic. I can show you around and introduce you to the cool peeps.'

'What about Chad?' I asked, with just a tinge of acid in my tone. After hooking Chad so quickly, was she going to just drop him now? Talk about catch and release.

'Chad?' She looked at me blankly.

'Yeah, you know, the new guy you were so keen to be with at the party last night.'

114

For a microsecond she looked disconcerted and then she gave one of her laughs. How come I'd never noticed before how insincere they were?

She gave a flick of her hand. 'Really, Zoe, I talked to him for like a New York minute. I was just being friendly, that's all.' She turned back to Rion. 'So, are you going to try out for any of the sports' teams? If so, we might see each other a lot. I'm a cheerleader, you know.'

'Yeah, like Chelsea,' I said. But not like me. I was definitely not the cheerleading type. Not that I want to be, I told myself.

'I haven't decided,' Rion said. 'I'm not sure how long I'll be here yet. It depends on how long my uncle's going to be away. He's in the Brazilian rainforest at the moment on assignment.'

'Really? Sounds exciting. What does he do?' Jas asked.

'He's a journalist,' Rion said.

'He's a photographer,' I said at the same time.

Jas looked from one to the other, confused. We'd really have to get our stories straight.

'He's a photojournalist,' Rion said.

'You have the most awesome family, Rion,' Jas said. 'I'm dying to hear all about them.'

Time to go before we got caught in any more traps. I took out my phone and looked at it. 'Wow, look at the

115

time. We've got to get going.' I stood up and grabbed some of our bags.

'Certainly, Zoe,' Rion said and rose.

Jas's eyes were immediately drawn to Rion's feet. God, I forgot about those socks. I tried to stop the giggle that was trying to escape.

But Jas just said, 'Amazing socks, Rion. I just love that metrosexual look, so cool. I can see you're a trendsetter.'

Rion smiled. 'Thanks, Jas, that's so observant of you. Not everyone appreciates an original look.' Then he turned his head and winked at me.

He actually winked.

However was I going to survive this?

Chapter Eleven

'Welcome to East Valley High, Orion,' my maths teacher said as Rion came into class.

My mum had helped Rion to enrol, explaining to the school that it was only temporary until his uncle returned and he had the proper transfer forms and all. How she managed it, I don't know, but being a teacher herself she knew the right things to say.

Mum seemed to have taken to Rion, probably because he was smarmy, and as sweet to her as honey on toast. Even Dad seemed to like him now. Clearly he approved of the fact that Rion was polite and smart, and called him sir.

Last night I'd overheard Mum telling Dad that Rion was probably neglected, maybe even abused, and they shouldn't ask too many questions at this point because they might traumatise him. So far, so good, but I knew it couldn't last for long.

When Rion slid into a seat there was a flutter of interest, mainly from the girls. Even though he was wearing the dorky school uniform of a white shirt and grey trousers, which Mum had also managed to get for him, Rion still looked like every girl's fantasy.

Not that it affected me. I turned to the maths problems I was working on and ignored the whispered comments flying around me.

It turned out that Rion and I shared most of the same classes, except for physics, which my alien told me he absolutely 'adored'. Yep, that was his very word. I was still working on his vocabulary. And I was getting used to the queasy feeling I had when he was further than a hundred metres away. We worked out that as long as it wasn't too much further than that, we could manage.

Jas honed in on him as soon as maths class was over. 'Hey, Rion,' she said, 'isn't it great you're here.' She linked her arm through his, leading him away.

I didn't care. I knew Rion and I were both in the next class and I was glad of some alone time, however short it was. We had refined and gone over a few more details of his story last night, so hopefully he wouldn't get himself into any trouble with Jas or anyone else who asked him questions.

Just then Harry came up to me. 'Hi, Zoe, good party on Saturday, wasn't it?'

Considering the fact that hardly anybody had talked to poor Harry, and all he'd seemed to do was stand in a corner and eat pizza, I was surprised he thought that, but then I decided that he was probably just making conversation. After all, we'd known each other for years and I knew I was one of the few girls he felt comfortable talking to.

'Yeah, I guess,' I said, shifting my books to the other arm. Why did they have to make textbooks so heavy? It's not like many people were going to read them all or anything.

'I can take those for you, if you like.' Harry fell into step beside me. I noticed he was the same height as me now, and even though I wouldn't call him slim exactly, he had dropped a little weight so I figured he must have been having a growth spurt or something.

'That's okay,' I said, 'I can manage.'

'Yeah, Harry, she's probably twice as strong as you anyway,' Jack Casey said as he pushed by us.

I frowned at his back. Stupid jock. Then I turned back to Harry, who was trying to act all unconcerned and everything. 'Actually, this history book is getting on my nerves,' I said, and gave him the heaviest of my texts. I tried not to notice when he nearly dropped it.

We pushed through the crowds to my next class.

'So that new guy, hey, he seems nice,' Harry said.

Nice. That wasn't exactly the adjective I'd use for him. Frustrating, egotistical and opinionated maybe, and yeah, eye candy, not that it mattered to me. And sometimes, for a microsecond or two, he was bearable. But nice? Definitely not.

I shrugged. 'He's okay, I guess.'

'So he's staying with you?'

'For the time being,' I said, hoping it would be for a very short time. Surely his people had noticed by now that he wasn't in his normal state. I couldn't believe it could take years, like Rion had said, for them to start looking for him.

'You're not ...' Harry hesitated and turned kind of pink. 'You're not going out together or anything, are you?'

I almost laughed out loud at that one, and then I remembered that the reason my alien had turned into a real person in the first place was to make Chad Everett interested in me. Chad had totally ignored me in the one class we'd had that day, so I was sure that was never going to happen.

'Nah,' I said. 'We were just having some fun dancing together on Saturday. We're just friends.' And even that, I thought, was an exaggeration.

'Oh, that's good,' Harry said.

We were nearly at history class, which was a relief because Harry wasn't acting normally and it was starting to creep me out.

'I better have my book now,' I said.

But Harry was holding onto it tightly and shifting from one foot to another. 'Zoe, I was wondering ...'

'Don't stand in the doorway, Crosby, move,' Marko said as he brushed past us.

'Hey, Zoe, did you get that English homework done on the weekend? If so, can I borrow it at break?' Chelsea asked as she came up to us.

I shook my head. 'I was going to ask you the same thing,' I said.

Ms Bradbury's voice came from inside the classroom. 'I presume you people are eventually going to come into the classroom. Please don't let my lesson interrupt your conversations.'

'Oops, better go. Bradbury sounds in a fine mood, doesn't she?' Chelsea said as she went into the room

'Harry, book,' I said.

'Oh, sorry.' He finally gave me my history book.

I slipped into the classroom and saw Rion sitting in the front row, book open and pencil at the ready to write down every one of Ms Bradbury's pearls of wisdom. Ignoring him, I moved to the back, slid into a seat and prepared to be bored for the next fifty minutes.

By the end of the day, Rion had made himself popular with all of the female population of the school and most of the teachers he'd encountered. He was attentive and polite in class, wrote copious notes and answered questions correctly. Thankfully he didn't show off too much, but I'd warned him about that.

'Don't act like a know-it-all or you'll only draw attention to yourself,' I told him. 'They'll think you're a genius or something and want to test you, and before you know it they might figure out you're not, well, human.'

He'd seen the wisdom in that and for the most part followed my advice. He only corrected a teacher once or twice and even then he was polite. The teachers loved him.

But I was exhausted. I'd been constantly worried that he would say or do the wrong thing, and that our whole story would come apart like soggy Weet-Bix in a bowl of milk.

Jas had also been a pain. She'd hung around Rion all day so I never had a chance to talk to him privately and tell him what he should or shouldn't do. And it wasn't easy to lose her, even after school had ended.

'Rion, you should come with us after school to Macca's,' she said. 'Everyone will be there.'

Before he had a chance to answer, I said, 'No can do, Jas. We gotta go home straightaway. Mum has some stuff she wants us to do.'

I realised, of course, that Jas hadn't included me in that invitation. But she was going to have to understand that from now on was Rion and I were a pair. Wherever Rion went, I went, and we would never be more than a hundred metres from each other. I couldn't help grinning when I thought how that would upset Jas. And then I remembered, guiltily, that she was supposed to be one of my best friends.

But I was seeing her differently since Saturday night. Before then I hadn't noticed how manipulative and self-centred she was. Or maybe I had, but didn't care. I wondered if that was how I seemed to Rion. But more importantly, I wondered why I was feeling upset that Jas was hitting on Rion. After all, he was nothing to me.

'Oh come on, you can go for half hour or so,' Jas said to Rion. 'Zoe's mum doesn't get home from work until after four so she won't even notice. And I so want to talk to you about that history assignment we have to do. You seemed to know everything about the Second World War. Even Ms Bradbury was impressed.' She latched onto his arm and batted her baby blues at him.

For a moment I sensed he was wavering, actually wavering. Jeez, were *aliens* even affected by Jas as well as everyone else? Life was so unfair.

But then Rion seemed to come to his senses. He removed her hand, gave it a pat and said, 'Thanks for the invitation, Jas, but we do have a lot to do this afternoon. Some other time, perhaps.'

She gave a pretend pout. 'Okay, I'm going to hold you to that. Anyway, call me tonight. I wrote my number on your book.'

'Sorry, I don't have a phone,' he said.

She looked at him as if she could hardly believe his words.

'He broke it,' I said, and then grabbed his arm and started to walk away. 'We gotta go. See you tomorrow.' Unfortunately, I thought, as we made our escape.

We could have caught the bus, but I made sure we walked home. There was too much danger of the other kids asking Rion questions, and besides, it wasn't far. It was good exercise, burning up carbs and all that.

'Does she ever give up?' I complained as we headed down the street.

'She's just being friendly,' Rion said.

'Is that what you think?'

'Of course,' he said. 'Jas was very helpful in showing me where everything was at school, and she invited me to join the other students in a social setting, which is more than you did today, Zoe.' There was just the mildest accusation in his tone.

'I don't know how you can be so dumb,' I said.

'If by dumb you mean that I'm unable to speak, that's obviously not correct. If, however, you're using it in a more colloquial sense, as in not intelligent, I might remind you that I have an IQ in excess of three times the IQ of a human genius.'

How could these words come out of a guy that looked like Johnny Depp's son?

'Don't you realise that Jas is …' I searched for a word he would understand and then used one I knew he would get. 'She's smitten with you.'

He stopped and looked at me. He was clearly surprised, and more than a little shaken. 'Surely not.'

I smiled at the effect my words had had on him. 'Why do you think she's always hanging around you?'

'Because she's one of your friends and I'm always with you.'

'It's not *me* she wants to be with, Rion, it's *you*. When we see her she talks to you, not me. When we were in class together today she sat next to you, not me. And when she invited you to Macca's after school she wasn't including me in the invitation. What more proof do you need?'

'I think you're jumping to conclusions. As I said, she's just being welcoming.' Rion was having a serious case of denial.

I shook my head. 'Why is it so hard to believe she's attracted to you? You know you're good-looking. After all, that was part of the plan when you materialised, to look so hot that other boys would be jealous when you showed attention to me. Why does it surprise you that other girls are attracted to you?'

He smiled. 'So you think I look hot.'

I rolled my eyes. 'Totally missing the point here. You know you are. But if there's one thing you aren't, it's modest.' I started to walk again.

He caught up and swung into step beside me. 'Does it bother you?'

'What?'

'That Jas might like me, and I say *might* because I'm not convinced yet.'

'Whether you like Jas is more to the point,' I said, deliberately ignoring his question.

He thought for a moment and then said, 'I don't think that question is relevant because my people don't regard emotions as highly as human beings do. We don't engage in such trivialities.'

I couldn't help snorting. 'Well, that's the biggest lie you've told so far.'

'I hardly ever lie, except when absolutely necessary.'

I could see he was all offended like, which proved my point. 'Come on, Rion, you do too have emotions. You're getting all huffy and insulted now. And you're mega-conceited about how smart you are. That's an emotion. You've also shown you can be hurt. So don't give me that rubbish about not having emotions.'

'I never said we don't have them, I said we don't regard them as important. Quite honestly, dealing with human beings can be extremely frustrating and does occasionally cause one to express a mild form of pique.'

'Oh blah, blah, blah,' I said, feeling a tad frustrated myself.

'Blah, blah, blah? What kind of response is that?'

'Why don't you just answer the question? Do you like Jas or not?'

He gave a deep sigh. 'Since it seems to be so important to you I'll answer. She's acceptable. She's friendly, I believe she's attractive in the human sense, and she seems to appreciate my qualities.'

'Oh God, such a typical boy response,' I said. 'She's cute and she strokes your ego. Go on back to McDonald's, if you want. Just don't expect me to trail after you. I hope you get sick and choke on a burger.' I walked faster to get rid of him.

He let me go and that was good. I was even more fed up with this alien now, when he was a person, than when he'd been a bossy little bubble inside me.

I was nearly home when he caught up. 'Okay, I understand now. I know what the problem is.'

I turned to face him. 'Oh, do enlighten me.'

'You're jealous. I should've seen it before. After all, I recognised right from the beginning that you were attracted to me, although I hoped you were getting over it. And don't,' he said, taking a step back, 'try to retaliate physically because that will only prove it more.'

Obviously this alien could read body language clearly enough, even if he didn't have a clue about emotions. I was struggling to control mine.

'I'm not jealous and I'm not attracted to you,' I said after a few moments. 'But you're my responsibility and I don't want you to get into a situation you can't control. If you get involved with Jas, or anyone else for that matter, she'll find out what you are. That wouldn't be good at all.'

'But I wouldn't get involved with anyone, Zoe.'

'How can you be so sure of that?'

'Because I'm already involved with someone.'

Alarm bells started ringing inside me. How could this have happened so soon? And who had snatched Rion's attention without me even noticing. I had to ask. 'With who?'

'Why you, of course.'

Chapter Twelve

For a moment I was stunned into silence. This couldn't be happening. Rion had constantly pointed out how inferior I was compared to him and he had just said he didn't believe in emotions. I was totally confused.

'What do you mean?' We were now in front of my house and I stopped to look at him.

He bent his head, and dark hair drifted over his forehead. He flicked it back with a casual gesture. His dark eyes looked into mine and I felt the smallest flutter. It was so hard to believe he was an alien at times. Especially when he didn't speak.

'Isn't it obvious?' he said.

'Not to me it isn't.' I wished he would stop looking at me with that intense stare. It was unnerving.

'We're bonded for life, Zoe. Hopefully I won't always have this form, but I'll be with you until you die. There's nothing either of us can do about that.'

'Oh that,' I said. Same old, same old, I thought. Why had I ever imagined it was anything else? Good to know that everything was normal—well, as normal as they could be when you were bonded to an alien for life.

He crinkled his brow. 'What did you think I meant?'

'Nothing,' I answered quickly.

We walked up the path and automatically we both sat down on the front steps. I rested my back on the step behind me and put down my books.

'I believe we need to talk about this,' Rion said, also leaning back, copying my actions.

'About what?'

'Relationships. They seem to be very important to human beings, especially those who are adolescents.'

I wasn't sure I liked where this conversation was heading. 'Nothing to talk about as long as you stay clear of them, Rion, it just wouldn't work out.'

'I agree with you totally and there's no worry about that happening with me. Your species is so inferior to my race that it would be impossible—and wholly undesirable.'

'Gee, thanks,' I said. Yep, I thought, totally attractive as long as he kept his mouth shut, but after that it was all downhill.

'You're welcome. No, I was thinking about relationships *you* might have. When I was part of your consciousness I was willing to accept your interest in boys, and even, as you know, help you. I need hardly add that's why I'm in my present predicament. However, now that I have a physical form it's more complicated.'

'Still not getting it,' I said.

He heaved a heavy sigh. 'Do I have to spell it out for you, Zoe? It will be very difficult for you to have any sort of relationship with a member of the opposite sex while I'm in this present state. For one thing, we need to keep in close proximity to each other, and for another ...'

'Yes?' An ominous feeling was coming over me.

'It would be very uncomfortable for me. I don't share your thoughts any more, which I must say is a relief because I was finding the thoughts of a fifteen-year-old girl tedious at times, but I do still infer from your moods what you're thinking. If you were to have a boyfriend at this stage I'd find it quite exhausting. All those emotional ups and downs, the constant drama ... I couldn't deal with it. Considering how young you are, I think it wise if you wait a year or two until my people have resolved the issues about my having a physical body and I can return to my previous state. After that, it will be easier. I've learned, over the lifetimes of the many people I have inhabited, how to put myself into deep meditation so I can have a rest from the tumultuous lives of human beings. I haven't quite mastered that ability in this physical state. I believe that being human weakens me and my abilities.'

I sat up. 'You've got to be joking. Are you telling me I can't have a boyfriend for years because it would inconvenience you? Not happening, you selfish, self-entitled alien.'

'No need to be offensive.' He was starting to look huffy and oversensitive as he always did when he heard a few home truths.

'Offensive? I haven't even started. And what do you think you are? Every second sentence you say insults me, and my "human state", as you call it. Now listen up. I'm going to have as many boyfriends as I want, when I want. Yes, you'll have to keep your distance, but a hundred metres will be enough. That's half the length of the school oval. Most houses are smaller than that. And as for my "tumultuous" emotions, get over it. You're here to learn about human beings, so start learning. It's not all facts and figures and dry old textbooks. No wonder your people are taking so long to work us out. Being human means having emotions, and the sooner you learn that, the quicker you'll learn what makes us tick. Finally, I'm nearly sixteen and smarter than you in some ways. At least I know when I've overstepped boundaries, something you've never learned.'

I stood up. 'And now I'm going to my room. I don't want to see you or talk to you or have anything to do with you until we have to meet for dinner. Till then, leave me alone.'

I climbed the couple of steps to the front door, let myself in and didn't bother to stop the screen door from slamming behind me.

Once I got to my room, I flung myself on the bed and burst into tears. Why I was crying I really didn't know. Was it because I was 'bonded' for life to this alien, a depressing enough thought, or was it because Rion had so little regard for me? There'd been moments when I'd almost liked him, when I'd almost thought of him as human, and maybe even someone I could be friends with. But it was obvious he didn't consider me anything other than 'an inferior species'. Strangely, that hurt.

I stayed in my room for the rest of the afternoon, trying to distract myself by fiddling on my phone, checking Facebook and texting a couple of friends. I even did some homework, anything to distract me from thinking about aliens, specifically the one I was sharing my life with.

When it was time for dinner, I washed my face just in case there was any sign that I'd been crying, changed into a clean T-shirt and jeans since my school uniform was all wrinkled from lying down, and spritzed myself with Mum's best perfume, just to make myself feel better.

I went to set the table, which was my usual job in the evening.

'Hi, darling, how was your day? Where have you been all afternoon?' Mum looked up from the books she was correcting at the end of the dining table.

Dad was in the kitchen making what smelled like lasagne. It was his turn to cook tonight, thank goodness. I took comfort from the fact that my mum would never be on *Master Chef* or *My Kitchen Rules*. Dad wasn't much better, but his lasagne was passable. Occasionally I took a turn, mostly on weekends, and even my parents agreed I wasn't too bad. The hopeless-in-the-kitchen gene wasn't passed onto me.

'I was in my room doing homework.' I took the placemats from the sideboard and started putting them on the table. Mum shifted some of her books to make room for me.

Dad popped his head around the corner. 'Am I hearing correctly, or has an alien inhabited my daughter's body?'

I nearly dropped the placemat I was holding.

'Rion must be having a good influence on you,' Mum said, and smiled.

It was all I could do not to say a totally inappropriate word.

'How did he go today?' Dad asked, coming into the dining room. There was a spot of sauce on his tie and a dripping wooden spoon in his hand.

'Fine, I guess.'

I took the spoon from him and went into the kitchen to get the cutlery. I was in no mood to talk about my alien. I dropped the spoon in the sink and took out the cutlery from the drawer. When I came back in, Rion had come downstairs and was talking to Mum and Dad, all smiles and politeness. I ignored him and carried on setting the table.

He looked over at me. 'May I help you, Zoe?'

'I've got it,' I said, trying hard not to plonk the knives and forks down with a clatter.

During dinner Rion was Mr Perfect, schmoozing my parents with his stories of school and lying about how much he'd liked it and everyone he'd met. I said as little as possible.

'It sounds as if you've settled in well,' Mum said, looking pleased.

'Have you thought about joining any sports teams?' Dad asked.

I wondered how Rion, who had never caught or kicked a ball, let alone done anything resembling sport at all, would get out of that one.

He pretended to consider the question for a moment and then said, 'I like cricket, so maybe I'll sign up if I'm still here in the spring.'

Dad nodded, satisfied with the answer. 'Yes, no doubt your uncle will be back by then. But since he lives near by he'll probably keep you at the same school.'

The words 'if I'm still here' gave me some hope. Maybe Rion was reconsidering his options. But it was time to change the subject before Dad started to ask any more questions about Rion's 'uncle'.

'Any dessert?' I asked.

'I made a rather nice chocolate mousse yesterday,' Mum said.

'On second thoughts, I'm fine thanks,' I said, knowing better than to say yes to anything my mum had made. I'd been hoping for ice cream or something from the shop.

'Well, since you've gone to the trouble of making it, of course,' Dad said bravely.

To my surprise, Rion also said yes. Were there any lengths he wouldn't go to in order to suck up to my parents?

'You do realise there's a lot of sugar in chocolate mousse?' I couldn't resist saying to Rion. It was the first time I'd talked to him directly during the meal.

He smiled at me. 'I'm sure it'll be fine, Zoe. After all, it is homemade.'

He'd have to do more than smile if he thought I was going to get over this afternoon.

'Since when have you ever worried about sugar?' Dad said as Mum went out to the kitchen to get the dessert.

'I'm very health conscious, Dad. I've actually learnt a lot about nutrition, especially lately.'

'Oh, from one of your teachers?' Dad asked.

'I guess you could say from an expert. He seems to know lot about absolutely everything, at least in his opinion.' I had the satisfaction of seeing Rion turn red. How interesting. I didn't know aliens could blush.

Mum came in with the dessert, and conversation stopped for a while everyone coped with chocolate mousse that resembled brown, lumpy mud. I looked at Rion and was surprised to see him enjoying it. He actually had seconds. It made me seriously question the food choices of aliens. What did they normally eat? Bugs?

After dinner I got up to clear the dishes and stack the dishwasher, another one of my nightly chores. Rion rose, too, and started to clear the table.

'You don't need to do that. I can manage. I'm sure you must have homework to do,' I said.

'Actually, I've completed it.'

Of course he had.

'No need to put on an act for the parents,' I said. 'They've gone.' Dad had drifted off to watch television and Mum had gone upstairs for a shower. I swished past him into the kitchen.

He trailed after me, laden with the rest of the plates. 'It's not an act, Zoe. I'm happy to help.'

I whirled around to face him. 'But I don't want your help. The only thing I want is for you to be gone.'

He carefully put the plates on the counter and then turned back to me. 'You're still angry with me.'

'What was your first clue?'

He started to speak and then stopped. 'That was a rhetorical question, wasn't it?' he said after a moment. 'I'm sorry to have upset you. I said some things that I now realise were hurtful. I seem to do that a lot. I'm not always diplomatic. That has been a criticism from some of my other hosts, too.'

Surprise, surprise, I thought.

'You made some valid points. There's much about being human that I still don't understand. I know I said I would try to learn some of these things from you.'

'You mean from such an 'inferior' being as me?'

He moved towards me and put his hands on my arms. Looking down at me, he said, 'I shouldn't have said that. You're right, I do overstep boundaries at times, and I can be arrogant. Perhaps I'm not as perfect as I like to think. I'm sorry, again. It seems that I make a lot of mistakes.'

I bit back the sarcastic remark that wanted to escape. I could be gracious and forgiving. 'Okay,' I said, 'apology accepted.'

He dropped his hands and smiled. 'Thank you.'

I started stacking the dishwasher and he began to pass me dishes. He was determined to help, whether I wanted it or not. For a few minutes we worked in harmony.

'Perhaps we need to do more things together so we can understand each other better,' he said.

'You mean that spending every waking moment together isn't enough?' I said as I took the last plate and closed the door of the dishwasher.

'We're near each other physically, but we don't do much together except have disagreements,' he said, wiping down the kitchen bench.

I started the machine and then took a paper towel to wipe up some spots of sauce that were still on the floor. Dad was not a neat chef. Straightening up, I threw the paper towel in the bin. Maybe Rion had a point. Even I was getting tired of arguing.

'Okay,' I said, 'what do you suggest we do?'

'Something enjoyable,' he said, leaning against the pantry door. 'Something fun.'

Now there was a word I never thought I'd hear him say. It would be kind of interesting to see how he'd act in a social situation.

'There's another party we could go to this weekend, if you want to. It probably won't be as good as last week's because Caitlyn's parents are going to be there, but it might be okay.' Even as I said the words, I realised I didn't want to go. As soon as Jas learnt that Rion would be at the party, she'd go too and I may as well stay home.

But to my surprise, Rion said, 'I don't want to go out with other people, just you.'

'So, kind of like a date?' I said, and smirked because it so wasn't going to be like that. He wasn't Chad Everett. Heck, he wasn't even Harry Crosby, who at least was human.

But Rion answered quite seriously, 'Yes, that's it. We'll go on a date.'

Chapter Thirteen

Okay, honestly? I've never had a boyfriend. Embarrassing, I know, especially since I was two months away from turning sixteen. Sure, I'd had a few kisses. The first was in year seven at Casey Short's birthday party when we played spin the bottle, and that was Casey himself. Not a promising start, especially since he was wearing braces.

Since then I'd been on dates, of course, and I'm not saying there hasn't been a bit of making out involved, but not much and it's never led anywhere. So naturally I exaggerated my experience to the other girls. Well, to be honest, I lied. If Jas had known the extent of my 'experience' there was no way we could've been friends. She only hung out with cool people.

This year I'd been determined to change that. I was going to have a boyfriend. For a while, a very short while,

Chad Everett had looked like a promising candidate. But even when it became obvious that Jas wasn't that into him—pretty much as soon as she'd seen Rion—he hadn't looked at me. Nope, didn't happen. And there weren't any other likely prospects at the moment.

So when Rion said I shouldn't have any relationships for a while, it was kind of ironic (a word I'd learned from him) because there wasn't much chance of that happening in the near future. And maybe that was another reason I got so upset. It was kind of like rubbing salt into the wound.

But after our talk, Rion and I got along much better. Over the next few days he hardly ever boasted about how clever he was. Well, only about once or twice a day, which was a big improvement over the several dozen times it used to happen. And he never put me down—at least not intentionally. Rion was trying hard to fit in, and not just with me but with everyone else as well.

He still spoke like   swallowed a dictionary but, amazingly, everyone thought it was kind of cute, especially the girls. So, going on a pretend date with Rion was about the closest I would get to looking normal to my friends. But I hadn't meant to give the impression that Rion and I were anything more than friends—until I kind of got fed up with their attitude. Well, to be specific, Jas's.

'It's so awesome that Rion's kind of nerdy like those guys on that TV show that are scientists, except he's better looking,' Chelsea gushed after school one day. 'You're so lucky he's staying with you.' She gave me a speculative look. 'Anything going on between you two?'

Jas joined us. 'Of course not,' she said. I was just about to agree with her when she added, 'You're not really his type, are you Zoe?'

I was getting tired of the way Jas treated me. Things had definitely cooled between us. She hadn't called me since the party on Saturday night, and now she was hinting that I wasn't good enough to be with someone like Rion.

So I said, 'As a matter of fact, we're going out on a date this weekend.'

Jas looked at me for a moment, and not in a friendly way.

'I knew it,' Chelsea said.

'Yeah, I'm not sure where we're going yet, but Rion said he doesn't want to hang out with anyone else, just me.' I was on a roll.

Jas shrugged. 'I guess staying with your parents, and you being around him all the time, doesn't give him much chance to get to know anyone else. He's probably just being nice, Zoe. I wouldn't get your hopes up if I was you.'

I was beginning to wonder why Jas and I had ever become friends in the first place. We'd only really become close this year, and that was because my best friend, Mandy Dover, had moved to Sydney at the end of last year. I'd decided to try to get into Jas's group because they were cool. It took me most of first term, but I finally made it and after that my social life had looked up—for a while. Now I wasn't so sure.

'I might say the same to you, Jas,' I said. The moment the words came out of my mouth, I knew it was a mistake. Nothing good ever came from antagonising Jas.

Her eyes narrowed and her hand came up to her waist. 'Seriously? You want to go there? If it wasn't for me letting you into our group this year, you'd still be hanging out with losers like Harry Crosby.'

Unfortunately, it was just as this moment that poor Harry came by. He hurried past us and out of the school grounds, pretending he hadn't heard, but I saw his face.

Before I had a chance to say anything, Rion came up. 'Are you ready to go home, Zoe?'

More than ready. I was already wishing I hadn't said anything to the girls about our 'date'. Rion, who was annoyingly honest at the wrong times, might let them know it was a friendship date and not the real thing. That would so not do my reputation any good.

'Yeah, sure,' I said.

'Hey, Rion, I just loved how you corrected Mr Law in class today about that point in physics. But you were so polite when you did it, *très* cute.' Jas gave him a simpering look.

Physics was the one class Rion and I didn't share, so I hadn't been able to give him death stares to remind him to be quiet. And as for Jas, could she have been any more obvious?

'I only meant to point out an alternative theory to the one he was teaching us,' Rion said, in a false attempt to sound humble.

'I honestly think you know more than he does,' Jas said.

'Yeah, totally,' Chelsea added. If she had to pick sides between Jas and me, I knew which one she'd pick.

'Oh, I just had a thought,' Jas said. 'I'm really struggling with this physics homework. I don't suppose you could help me, Rion. I'd be so grateful.' She batted her baby blues at him, and if he'd been a real guy she would've had him hooked, or at least interested.

'Yes, of course,' Rion said. At times he was inconveniently polite.

'Great. Could you come over like this afternoon? I want to get it done now, you know, as I have about a billion other assignments and stuff to do. I so hate being late with homework,' Jas lied.

Then she turned to me with a sickly smile. 'Zoe, you don't mind, do you? You're not in physics class. That's mainly for the A-stream students.'

As if the universe wasn't already on her side, she was actually reasonably smart as well as beautiful, popular and rich. So unfair. I knew she didn't need Rion's help at all. I was beginning to really dislike my former friend, but I knew the challenge was on. Jas wasn't likely to let anything she wanted slip out of her grasp, whether it was an expensive pair of shoes or a boy. Luckily, I had an ace up my sleeve that she didn't know about.

'Gee, your house is several kilometres from mine, isn't it? It's not like it's a hundred metres or so down the street,' I said.

She looked at me as if I was slightly nutty.

Rion, however, grasped the situation immediately. But he also had a solution. 'Why don't you come over to Zoe's house?' he asked Jas. 'It's not that far and it won't take us long to go through the homework.' Sometimes he was altogether too clever for my liking.

I could see that Jas wasn't too keen on his suggestion either. 'It'll be much quieter at my place,' she said, 'because no one's there. We don't want to get in the way of Zoe or her mum when she comes home.'

'Zoe and her mum won't mind.' He looked at me and smiled.

'Sure, come on over, Jas,' I said.

It was better than the alternative, and that way I'd be there to keep an eye on things. Not that I cared or anything, but Rion and I had already agreed that relationships wouldn't be a good idea. And Jas was seriously getting on my nerves.

She pursed her lips and I could tell there were about a million thoughts racing through her mind. Then she shrugged and said, 'Okay, but let's catch the school bus. It's due any moment and it's too hot to walk, though you can if you want, Zoe.'

It was winter, and even though it was a Queensland winter where the temperature rarely made single digits, it was by no means hot. She just wanted to get Rion away from me.

'Sure, we can get the bus,' I said.

There was no way I was going to let her win this one, and besides, Rion on the bus and me walking would make me feel ill, in more ways than one. Chelsea, who was being picked up by her mum, said goodbye. I knew that she and Jas would be on the phone tonight talking over the day's events. By tomorrow I'd probably be out of their group—if I weren't already.

So the three of us piled on the bus, and of course Jas managed to get a seat for her and Rion, forcing me to sit somewhere else. She was good, I had to give her that.

When we reached home I told Rion that he and Jas could have the dining table. 'Mum's at a staff meeting today and won't be home for ages,' I said. 'I'm sorry you can't use the study at the moment, but Dad's got some tax stuff all over the desk.' No way did I want them in there with the door closed.

But Jas came up with an even more unacceptable idea. 'I don't want to take over your house or anything. Why don't we go to your room, Rion? It'll be so much quieter and easier to concentrate.'

Rion looked from me to Jas, clearly struggling to decide what was the right thing to do. But Jas took the matter in hand by going upstairs and leaving Rion to trail behind her.

I sighed. Whatevs. I told myself that Rion was such a literal person he would just help her with the homework and then get rid of her, if he didn't bore her with science facts before then.

I headed to the kitchen for a snack. Maybe digging out the milkshake maker would be a good idea. I was in the mood for a double-choc milkshake, heavy on the ice cream. I needed—no, I *deserved*—a sugar hit.

Halfway through my milkshake, a sneaky little thought entered my mind. Why couldn't I be a good hostess and make a milkshake for Rion and Jas, too? Then I could legitimately knock on Rion's door and interrupt them. Wouldn't Jas love that? Not.

So I made the most fattening, sugar-loaded and delicious milkshakes I could for the weight-obsessed Jas and the health nut Rion. What a wicked but clever brain I had.

It was tricky balancing two death-by-chocolate milkshakes on a tray and knocking on Rion's bedroom door at the same time, but I managed.

After a few moments Rion opened the door. His shirt was slightly untucked and his hair uncharacteristically ruffled. He had a look on his face that could have been guilt or just unease. What on earth was going on in there?

'Hi,' I said, 'just brought you up a snack.'

I walked into the room and saw Jas sitting on the floor, legs crossed and looking very pleased with herself.

'So sweet, but I don't usually eat before dinner,' she said. 'Rion and I are busy, anyway. He's been so helpful.' She smiled up at him.

I set the milkshakes down on his desk.

'Thanks, Zoe,' Rion said. 'That was very thoughtful of you.'

'I thought you could do with an energy boost,' I said. 'Why don't you try it and see if you like it?'

I could see that Rion was again struggling between politeness and an obvious desire to give me yet another lecture on the dangers of sugar and fats. Politeness won out. He picked up a glass and handed it to Jas, who could hardly refuse since it was Rion who was giving it to her. And then he picked up the other glass and drank a little. I fully expected him to put it down again, but instead he took another even bigger sip.

'This is actually very nice,' he said. 'You should try it, Jas.'

She took a sip and grudgingly said, 'Not bad.'

I was an expert milkshake maker.

'Are you two nearly finished with the homework?' I said.

'Not at all,' Jas said, 'there's heaps more Rion needs to explain to me. We might even have to get together tomorrow.'

Rion looked puzzled. 'But we've gone over your homework.'

'You were starting to explain the theory of relativity to me,' Jas said. 'It was so interesting. Mr Law never makes our lessons so cool.'

'I must admit physics is a fascinating subject,' Rion said.

'And you're so clever in making it all easy to understand,' Jas said.

His face lit up. At that moment Rion seemed just as dumb as any other guy. I wondered again why he'd seemed so guilty when he opened the door. What had Jas been up to? Maybe it was time for me to mount a rescue operation.

'My mum will be home soon. Didn't you say you were going to help her make dinner tonight, Rion?'

This time he really did look guilty. 'Oh, I forgot about that.'

'We have to finish these milkshakes you made for us first, though,' Jas said, lifting the glass and her eyebrow. She knew what I was doing.

'Sure.' I sat down on the bed. 'I'll take the glasses when you're finished.'

'No need,' Rion said, being ever helpful. 'I can do that.'

'Yeah, why don't you go down and get things started for your mum, Zoe,' Jas said. 'She'd appreciate that. 'We'll be down in a few minutes.'

Left with no choice, I went out, but I left the door open behind me. I heard it close as I went downstairs. I cleaned up the mess I'd made in the kitchen and then peeled the vegetables for dinner. It was twenty-seven minutes before they came down. Not that I was timing them or anything. I just happened to notice the clock.

I heard Jas's syrupy tones. 'Thanks so much, Rion, everything makes so much more sense than before. Now, don't forget we're meeting for lunch tomorrow at school to go over a few more things. You sure you can't walk to the bus stop with me? It's getting kind of dark.'

'Sorry, but I really need to help with the dinner now. But I'm sure Zoe will walk with you if you're nervous.'

I popped my head around the corner of the kitchen as they walked to the front door. 'Sure,' I said, 'no probs, Jas. I'm not afraid of the dark.'

'That's all right, I'll be fine.' Acid poured from those words.

'Okay. A walk will give you a chance to work off those calories from that double cream and extra-chocolate milkshake. Hope you enjoyed it. Byeee.' I said. What was wrong with me? I wasn't usually like this.

I think the front door might have closed more forcibly than usual as she left. So that was it. We had definitely moved from friends to enemies.

All this, of course, went totally over Rion's head. He didn't have a clue about human relationships, especially when it came to teenage girls.

When he joined me in the kitchen I said, 'So, what happened?'

He looked at me with a blank expression. 'What do you mean?' He rinsed the milkshake glasses he'd brought down. They were both empty, I noticed.

'Between Jas and you.'

'I helped her with her homework. You knew that.'

I picked up a tea towel to dry the glasses. 'And what else?'

He sighed. 'You actually want to know everything that happened?'

'Yes,' I said as I put the glasses away and turned to face him, folding my arms. 'Everything.'

'We talked about the theory of relativity. I always envied the being that had inhabited Einstein. I really wanted him as a host.'

'Are you telling me that Einstein was inhabited by one of you aliens?' I shook my head in disbelief. 'Never mind. Don't want to get distracted here. Go on.'

'Then you came up with the milkshakes and we drank them and now Jas has gone. But you know all this. Why are you asking me?' He looked genuinely puzzled.

'That's not all. You're leaving something out. You looked all … dishevelled when I came up.' I had to admit that Rion was improving my vocabulary.

He turned a little red. 'Well, now that you mention it, Jas did get a little physical. She seems an affectionate kind of girl.'

I felt my eyes narrowing, 'What do you mean?'

'She, um, kissed me,' Rion said.

I knew it. Just as I was about to ask for details, I heard the front door open.

'Hi Zoe, Rion. I'm home.' Mum's voice sang through the hallway.

Chapter Fourteen

Mum came into the kitchen carrying a couple of grocery bags, which Rion immediately took from her and started to unpack.

'Thanks, Rion,' Mum said. 'Oh, you've already started preparing dinner. How thoughtful of you.'

No doubt about it, if my mum had had a son, she would have wanted one exactly like Rion.

'It was Zoe who did this,' he said truthfully.

'Thanks, dear,' Mum said to me, and laughed. 'Looks like I could almost retire from this cooking business.'

I did not say a word, though I was tempted. I had other things on my mind, like Jas and that kiss. I wanted details and I wanted them now.

Mum took off her cardigan, put it on the back of a chair and went to wash her hands. 'Now, let's get this vegetarian lasagne started.'

'Why don't you get a glass of wine and sit down, Mum?' I said. 'I'm sure you must be tired, especially after a day's teaching and that long staff meeting. Rion and I will make dinner. In fact, why don't you have a shower, too? It'll make you feel refreshed.'

Mum looked at me in surprise. 'What is this, Mother's Day?'

'Can't I be nice to my mum occasionally? Besides, it'll give me brownie points for when I really want something.'

'Hmm, what is it, Zoe? Tell me now.'

'Nothing … yet.' I gave her a wide grin and a gentle push towards the door. 'I think Dad bought a nice Shiraz yesterday.'

She turned her head to look at me and quirked an eyebrow. 'How do you know so much about wine, missy?'

'I'm just incredibly observant, Mum.'

She shook her head. 'I don't believe that for a moment, but I'm too tired to argue. All right, since you insist I will go and relax. That professional-development session after school was yet another meeting that could've been an email.' She left the kitchen and headed upstairs, finally.

Rion had already opened the cookbook to the recipe we were using, turned on the oven and had all the ingredients we needed on the kitchen counter. 'Would you grate two cups of cheese, Zoe?' he said. 'I'll get the sauce started.'

Did he seriously think we were just going to get on with the cooking after that bombshell he'd just dropped?

'Sit down, Rion. We need to talk.'

'What about?'

Jeez, was he really that innocent? 'Are you serious? You just told me that you kissed Jas.'

'Correction. She kissed me,' he said, and sat down across from me.

'So how did that happen? I thought you weren't into this emotion stuff. Didn't even think you liked Jas in that way.' I knew, of course, that it was all Jas's doing. I should never have left them alone.

He shifted in his chair, pushed away the dark lock of hair that had fallen over his forehead and clasped his hands together on the kitchen table. I had never seen him look so uncomfortable.

'I don't quite know how it happened,' he said. 'And you're right. I'm not into this "emotion stuff", as you call it. I really don't know how you humans cope. It's very unsettling and not at all pleasant.'

157

I couldn't argue with that. My emotions were anything but settled and pleasant at the moment. I waited for him to continue.

'We were sitting on the floor because there wasn't enough room at the desk.'

'Told you it would've been better to use the dining-room table.'

'I see that now but she didn't give me much choice.'

'That's Jas for you,' I said. I used to admire her determination and ability to sweep everything and everyone else aside in order to get what she wanted. Now, not so much. 'Go on,' I said.

'She kept leaning against me while we were looking at the text. At first I didn't think anything of it, but it became uncomfortable so I moved away. And then—'

'She moved next to you again,' I said, finishing his sentence.

He looked at me in surprise. 'Exactly. How did you know? Anyway, I was in the middle of an explanation about the last question when she put a finger on my lips—which I thought was a little rude, by the way—and then leaned towards me. Before I could move again she took her finger away, put her lips on mine and kissed me. It was an unusual sensation.'

'And then what happened?' I asked, though I wasn't sure I wanted to know.

'You knocked on the door and I got up and let you in.'

No wonder he'd looked so confused when he answered the door.

'So did she try to kiss you again after I left?' There was nothing I'd put past Jas, but surely she must have realised Rion just wasn't that into her. Or was he?

'I sat on the chair next to my desk and we finished the drink you made for us. It was really quite delicious, by the way. I did try to go over the basic elements of Einstein's theory, but she either didn't understand or had lost interest. Right in the middle of my explanation she got up and put her glass on the desk next to mine, and then she sat on my knee. Why, I'm not sure, because it really wasn't very comfortable. Besides, I knew I needed to help you with dinner. So I lifted her off and said it was time she left.'

I hid a smile. That must have pleased her, not.

'So that's it,' Rion said, sounding relieved. 'Shall we continue with the preparations for dinner?'

But I wasn't quite finished. There were still a couple of things I wanted to know. 'So, just curious, how did you feel when she kissed you? Did you like it?'

He thought for a moment. 'It was strange. I've never been kissed before. Once we become pure consciousness and join a mothercloud we don't usually materialise into a physical form, so our experiences are limited in that way.' He smiled.

'Yeah, limited, got it. What else did you think about that kiss?'

'It wasn't unpleasant, although I tried not to think of all the germs that could be passed from one person to another in that way. Kissing is probably not very hygienic.'

It amazed me again how someone who looked liked Rion could talk like that. 'So, how long did this kiss last?'

'You're asking a lot of questions about this. Have you never been kissed, Zoe? Is that why? Are you seeking information about it?'

'Ahhhh! Honestly Rion, you test my patience. How can you know so little about human beings? Hard to believe you've clocked up over four thousand years here. Were you asleep most of that time? Of course I've been kissed. Not that it's any of your business.'

'Interesting.' He was looking at me in a thoughtful manner.

'What?'

'You want to know every detail of my kiss with Jas, but you think I have no right to ask about your own physical encounters.'

'It's different,' I said. No way was I going to tell him about the very few times I'd been kissed. Jeez, I didn't even share with the girls about how lame most of those times were. I was still waiting for that one kiss that would be amazing. Or that one boy.

'I fail to see how it's different,' he said.

'You're an alien and I have to look out for you, especially around people like Jas.'

'Okay, thank you, but I don't see the point. Perhaps you can help me by telling me what your experiences have been. That way I'll be more prepared.'

'You don't need to be prepared because it's not going to happen again. And I am so not telling you about when boys kissed me, so forget it.'

'Hmm, not an adequate or a logical explanation, but we'll leave it for now. I am curious, though. Perhaps I need to discover these things for myself.'

'What do you mean?' I didn't like the way this conversation was heading.

'Purely in the interest of scientific research, I may do some experiments.'

'What experiments?' I asked in alarm.

'I may just have to try this kissing thing again,' he said. His mouth quirked up and his eyes met mine.

I couldn't work out if he was teasing me or deadly serious. He was so hard to read sometimes. But just to be on the safe side, I said, 'The germs, Rion, think of the germs. You really don't want to catch a deadly disease or anything.'

I heard Mum coming down the stairs again. Any minute now she would probably pop in to see how we were going with dinner. And it was definitely time to change the topic.

Rion must have read my mind. 'Let's get cooking, shall we?' he said.

I got up and grabbed the cheese and the grater while Rion started on the sauce. We worked in silence for a while and there was kind of an uncomfortable vibe in the air. I had felt many different emotions with this alien, but I had never felt quite this way. I wished, for about the hundredth time, that I hadn't been on that beach the day he decided to fall down from the air and land on his next human.

In the middle of all this feeling weird and also sorry for myself, I was careless and dropped the cheese grater on the floor. Before I could get it, Rion bent down, picked it up, dusted the shavings of cheese off in the sink and handed it back to me.

'What, aren't you going to sterilise it?' I said in surprise. 'Or rush out and buy a new one or something?' I knew how obsessive he was about these things.

There was that crooked little smile again. 'It'll be fine. I'm beginning to think there are worse things than a few germs here and there.' He turned back to the stovetop to stir his sauce.

Chapter Fifteen

I wondered how the friction between Jas and me would affect our friendship. Maybe I would be out of her group now, especially since I hadn't been in it very long and Jas definitely wasn't happy with me at the moment. I supposed I could go back to the friends I'd had before.

There was shy Lou Kennedy. And Kerri O'Reilly, whose grades never dropped below an A. And Harry Crosby. My best friend Mandy, who had moved away, had also been in our old group. After Mandy left I didn't have any other close friend, and so when Jas invited me to join her group it seemed like a good idea. They were definitely the cool kids. Suddenly party invitations had started coming my way, and I hoped that cool boys would, too. I was still waiting for that last thing to happen.

My old group might not even want me back. Feelings had been a bit hurt when I abandoned them, so I might end up in a group of one. High school was so complicated sometimes.

But then I thought of Rion. He would follow me, wouldn't he? He'd been accepted into Jas's group automatically, without even a trial run. That was partly because of me and partly because of him. But I had to be honest—it was *all* because of him, the hottest boy in our year level.

At lunchbreak I went outside and looked around at the seats, trying to decide where to sit. I was surprised when Jas called out.

'What are you doing, Zoe? We're over here.' She beckoned to me.

I went over and sat down next to the old fig tree, which was where her group always sat. It was their spot, and everyone else knew better than to take it. Everything seemed normal-ish. Jas sat on the seat and held court. Chad sat next to her, taking in her every word, and Chelsea, Jas's faithful minion, sat on the other side. The rest of us sat on the grass, and too bad about any green ants that might be lurking there. We knew our place.

I was surprised I was even welcome there again, especially after what had happened yesterday. But while

Jas wasn't overly friendly, she wasn't totally ignoring me either. Maybe I'd misjudged her and our friendship was stronger than I thought. I began to feel guilty about some of the things I'd said to her, not to mention what I'd thought about her.

Then Rion came over and sat next to me, and Jas lit up like a Christmas tree.

'Rion, what are you doing there on the grass?' she said. 'Come and sit next to me. Move over, Chad.'

Chad, looking anything but pleased, shuffled over to the edge of the seat. But Rion just shook his head and said, 'I'm fine, thanks.'

'Oh, don't be silly. No need to be shy, especially after yesterday,' Jas said, and gave a little giggle.

Had I misjudged her? I so had not. And now I realised why she hadn't kicked me out of the group. She was afraid Rion would follow me. Everyone looked from Jas to Rion, wondering what had happened between them, which was exactly what she intended. She threw them a crumb.

'I went over to Rion's yesterday and he helped me with my homework. I just love your bedroom, Rion. It's so cosy.' She twirled a strand of blond hair through her fingers. Interest heightened. 'I think I might need help with physics all this year. It really is a difficult subject and you explain it so well.'

'It also helps if you study,' I said. Sometimes I really should learn to keep my mouth shut.

She smiled at me sweetly. 'What a good idea,' she said, 'and who would've thought you'd come up with it, Zoe. That's just what I need, a study buddy. And I can't think of anyone better than you, Rion.'

Rion looked puzzled. 'I'm not sure what a "study buddy" is, but I'm happy to help if you or anyone else has problems.' He looked around the group.

Jas got up from her seat and plunked herself down beside Rion. Unheard of. She never moved for anybody.

'You're so cute, Rion,' she said, looking at him sweetly. 'I can't believe you don't know what that is. A study buddy is someone who helps you study, of course. It means we'll spend lots of time together, helping each other out. We could start this weekend. I have Saturday free, and afterwards we could catch a movie or something.'

If Jas said that to any other guy he would think all his Christmases had come at once. In fact, I could see Chad looking at Rion enviously. Chad would die for the chance to spend all that one-on-one time with Jas. But Rion wasn't just any other guy.

'Sorry, Jas,' he said, 'but I'm busy this weekend. On Saturday morning I'm helping Zoe's dad cut the grass, and later Zoe and I are going out on a date.'

He said it in a matter-of-fact tone, having no idea of the effect of his words. Even though I'd already told Chelsea and Jas about our date, I didn't think they'd really believed me. But they did now.

I tried really, really hard not to smirk. I tried to act cool. But inside I was kind of doing cartwheels. I felt my status go up instantly. Even Chad Everett was looking at me in a surprised kind of way.

Everyone knew my mum's habit of helping people. We once had a refugee lady stay with us for a week or two, and Mum was also in a couple of volunteer groups. So no one was surprised that Rion was staying with us. But no one expected him to give me a second glance. No one thought I was girlfriend material, at least not when it came to hot guys like Rion.

It might have taken a long time for Rion's plan to work, but it was finally having an effect.

Another reason I was feeling good was because Rion had actually told them. I knew it probably meant nothing to him because, after all, this was just a friendship date to help us get along better, but even after all the pressure from Jas he still wanted to go out with me. After yesterday, I'd wondered whether he'd want to hang around Jas a bit more to carry out those experiments in kissing.

'Oh,' Jas said. 'Of course you must have obligations and everything to Zoe and her family, seeing as you're staying with them. I totally understand. And Sunday is out for me. Family day.' She rolled her eyes. 'I know what it means to have to do stuff, too. But we'll work something out for next week.'

If anyone was good at saving face, it was Jas. Not that she had to do it very often. And she even managed to make it look like Rion was going on a pity date with me. It might have been a weak save, but it was a save nevertheless.

Rion nodded but said nothing.

Jas left soon after that. 'I've got a cheerleaders' meeting,' she said, and doing that flip thing with her hair, she added, 'Come on, Chelsea, we don't want to be late.'

The others drifted off, too, now that the centre of interest had gone. Soon only Rion and I were left.

'Thanks,' I said, brushing the crumbs of my sandwich off my lap and crinkling up the wrapping.

'For what?' Rion shifted on the grass so he was facing me.

'For telling the others that we're going on a date.'

'But we are, aren't we? You don't want to cancel it, do you?' He gave me his serious, puzzled look, which happened when he didn't understand human beings, which was pretty often.

'No, of course not,' I said. 'I thought you might, though, when Jas said she wanted to be with you.'

'Why would I do that?' Still that look.

'Because of, you know …' I suddenly had an unusual attack of shyness.

'No, I don't actually,' he said.

'Well, you told me last night that you wanted to try "this kissing thing" again. Jas would be more than willing and she is kind of hot.' I tried really hard to say that casually, but I felt my face get warm.

'Oh.' A look of understanding came over his face. He thought for a moment and then said, 'On closer inspection, I don't really think Jas is a person I admire.'

Now that did surprise me. He was in the minority there, both guys and girls. 'Really? Why?'

'I think, although I'm not sure because sometimes the subtleties of human interactions escape me, that she's not as nice and kind as she appears.'

'I'm not always nice or kind either,' I said.

'That's true.'

'Gee, thanks.'

'But you're honest. You don't say one thing and mean another. If you insult someone you don't hide it. I think Jas can be a little unkind at times.'

I was amazed that Rion had seen all of this. I knew he was smart with facts and figures and all that, but I didn't think he was smart about people. He was more observant than I gave him credit for.

'For example,' he said, 'I don't think she was very kind to you just then. She implied that my going out with you just was a social obligation. It isn't, you know.' He looked at me with his Zac Efron eyes and his crooked smile.

Okay, little bit of heart melting going on, even though it felt a bit weird. 'Isn't it?' I said in a kind of girly voice.

'No, of course not,' he said. 'You are, or were, my host. It's important that I know you so we can coexist together better when I eventually dematerialise. A mutually beneficial relationship is vital if we're to be linked together for the rest of your life.'

Jeez, I was tired of hearing about that bonding-for-life thing. And I really had to stop thinking about Rion as a human being. He was an alien, and that was something I couldn't forget.

'Yeah,' I said, 'of course.'

'So, what do you want to do this weekend?'

'Well, we could go to the movies.' That would involve minimal talking, and at the moment that suited me fine. I was feeling a bit over all of this.

'That's really just like watching television on a big screen, isn't it? It's not very interactive.'

I thought about alternatives. 'I guess we could go out for pizza or something.'

He shook his head. 'That seems superfluous since we can eat at home.'

'Jeez, Rion, I don't know. What do you want to do?'

He thought for a moment. 'I'd like to go bowling.'

'What? Where did you get that idea from?'

'I saw it on television. I think the program was called *Happy Days*. I think bowling would be fun.'

'You do realise that *Happy Days* is set in the nineteen fifties, don't you? Like last century. Things have changed a lot since then.'

'But they still have bowling alleys, don't they?'

'Yeah, I guess.' I had images of fat guys in bowling shirts, and older ladies in stretchy pants and floral shirts.

'Then let's try it out.' He gave me an enthusiastic smile.

'Sure, why not.' I shrugged. What difference did it make what we did? It wasn't like a real date or anything.

In last period I got yet another surprise. Rion was in physics, and I was in biology, the soft option for science, which was not my strongest area. We were in lab and making our second bisection of a frog. Gross, I know, but kind of interesting. This time we were looking at the liver. Who knew that it was so big in such a tiny creature. Anyway, Harry was my lab partner. Even though in real life Harry was kind of a klutz, he was good at this kind of stuff, and pretty smart, too. So I didn't mind him being my partner.

We'd examined the liver and made our observations. I copied some of Harry's notes into my science journal.

'You'll never be a doctor, you know that, Harry,' I said, looking up from my book.

He looked puzzled. 'Why? Not that I want to be or anything.'

'Because your handwriting is too neat,' I said, and laughed.

A lame joke, I know, but he laughed politely with me. That was one thing I liked about Harry. He was kind, even to people who didn't deserve it. And there were plenty of those who gave him a hard time. I didn't think I was one of them. Plus, I'd known him like forever.

When we cleaned up Harry started to act a bit awkward, dropping the magnifying glass and then bumping his head when he bent down to pick it up. He acted like this whenever he felt embarrassed or something. I wondered what was up.

Straightening, he put the magnifying glass back and then said, 'Um, Zoe.'

'Yeah,' I said, as I tidied up the rest of the things on our lab bench.

'I was wondering …'

'Mmm?' I put the frog back in the bucket of formaldehyde.

'Are you doing anything this Sunday?'

I shrugged. 'Don't think so.'

I knew Rion would probably bug me until I did my homework and, unlike Harry, he wouldn't let me cheat off him. Help, maybe, but he'd still make me do the work. I wondered if he'd done that with Jas. My mind wandered off and I was thinking of those things when Harry brought me back to the present.

'The thing is, I've got this party to go to. It's my cousin's eighteenth birthday and we're having a family barbecue. Would you like to go with me?' He looked at me, biting his lips and looking all anxious and hopeful at the same time.

'But isn't it kind of a family thing?' I asked. I had the awkward feeling Harry was asking me out on a date.

'Yeah, but they said I could bring someone. My mum could pick you up and drop you home. It'd be really cool if you could come.' His voice lifted a little.

'Did you tell them you were bringing someone, Harry?'

'I said I might,' he said, his voice trailing off.

I knew what that meant. His family was expecting him to bring a date, probably delighted that little Harry was growing up at last. I could just imagine what he'd feel like if he had to turn up alone and make up some excuse for why he didn't bring a girl. And I knew that if I didn't go nobody would.

I tried to keep down the big sigh that wanted to escape. Why, oh why, did I have to inherit the empathy gene from my mum? It was really inconvenient.

I looked at Harry and his hopeful, round face. 'Sure,' I said, 'what time?'

Chapter Sixteen

Most weekends I had zero dates. This weekend I had two. Go figure. Not that they were dates in the strict sense of the word. The one with Rion was just, well, who knows except it definitely wasn't a date in the boyfriend sense, and the one with Harry was, I had to admit, a pity date. I wasn't looking forward to either.

I mean, who wanted to go bowling? I thought it was either for little kids' birthday parties or old people's bowling leagues. It sure wasn't a cool activity. I just hoped no one would ask me where Rion and I had gone.

Mum and Dad thought it was a great idea for me to do something 'wholesome and healthy' rather than the parties I'd been going to all year. I knew they thought Rion was a good influence on me. I think they kind of hoped his uncle wouldn't come back for a long time.

This morning, for instance, Rion cut the grass, front and back, without even being asked. He was always doing stuff like that, taking in the washing off the line, putting out the rubbish, unstacking the dishwasher, even though that was my job, and his room was always anally tidy, unlike mine, which I felt had a more creative, unstructured vibe. Okay, it was untidy.

Rion was the ideal houseguest, and he wasn't going to wear out his welcome any time soon. So, no problem with him taking their one and only child out for the evening.

Putting on my second-best jeans and semi-nice blue top, I got ready for our date. I'd washed my hair and straightened it—with Mum's straightener now that I wasn't going to get one of my own for a while—and put on the barest minimum of makeup, just lip gloss and a hint of blush. I wasn't going overboard for bowling or, for that matter, Rion.

The bowling alley was just a short bus ride away, which was a plus because Mum wouldn't have to drop us there as if I was twelve.

'You look pretty, darling,' Mum said when I came downstairs. 'So nice to see you without all that makeup you usually cake on when you go out.'

'Glad to see you have something sensible on,' Dad said when he looked up from the paper he was reading in the lounge room. His idea of sensible was probably close to what the Victorians wore. 'Don't forget to take a cardigan,' he added. 'It's going to be cold tonight.'

Parents.

Rion was waiting at the door. He was wearing the jeans and brown T-shirt we'd bought at the mall, and his black jumper was knotted around his shoulders He looked, well … definitely not ugly. Too bad I knew that underneath that dreamy exterior was just a little soap-bubble alien whose mission in life seemed to be to make mine miserable. I'd be surprised if we got through this night without an argument.

He passed me the brown cable cardigan that I got two Christmases ago from an aunt who shall not be named. It was two sizes too big then and it was still loose now. Rion must have grabbed it from the broom closet where I'd stuffed it one day. It was really hard having three parents. But I took it anyway. Whatever. It's not as if I was out to impress or anything. Besides, the bus was due in a few minutes so we had to leave.

Rion was carrying a little white box in one hand. 'What's that?'

'I'll show you outside,' he said. Mysterious, much.

We said goodbye to the parents and left.

As we walked down the pathway, he put a hand on my wrist and stopped me. 'Okay, I'll show you what's in the box.' He opened the box, a little clumsily for him, and took out a small yellow flower. 'Here, this is for you,' handing it to me. 'I believe it's called a corsage. I used some of the money your father insisted on giving me today for mowing the lawn.'

I took it and looked at it in wonder. 'That's really nice of you, Rion, but I don't understand. Why did you get it?'

'I believe it's customary to give a girl one of these on a date. I did some research on the internet. You can either tie it on your wrist or pin it on your clothes. Since we're going bowling I thought perhaps you could put it on your cardigan.'

I tried really hard not to giggle. It was kind of sweet of him, but seriously, a corsage for a bowling date? Or any kind of date. This wasn't the 1960s or whenever it was that boys did stuff like this for fancy dances. Maybe they still did—somewhere—but they sure didn't do it for bowling. I felt like I should be wearing a big dress with about a dozen petticoats or crinolines underneath.

I wondered again what on earth Rion had learned in the many years he'd been here. Then I remembered that his last host had died at eighty-seven, which explained Rion's old-fashioned perspective on dating.

But I couldn't say any of this. He was looking all pleased with himself and I didn't have the heart to burst his bubble. 'Thanks, Rion, it's very pretty.'

'I had to improvise because they didn't have any corsages in the flower shop. I bought a large flower and used a little foil to wrap the stem. I also put in a pin. Here, let me attach it for you,' he said, beaming.

Gee, I actually had to wear it? Well, if Rion put it on the cardigan it meant I didn't have to wear it bowling because that brown woollen beast was coming off. So I let him pin the bright yellow flower on my daggy cardigan and even smiled. I *really* hoped there wouldn't be anyone I knew on the bus.

He stepped back and looked at it critically. 'Yes, I was right in thinking that your brown cardigan would go well with a yellow flower.'

'Um, yeah, sure, yellow and brown, I get it.' Not, I thought. My alien certainly didn't have a future ahead of him with Sass and Bide, or even Bettina Liano.

When we reached the bus stop we sat down to wait.

'You know you really didn't have to get me anything, Rion,' I said. 'It's not like this is a real date.'

'But I wanted to do it properly. I've started to realise how little I know about human interactions, so I thought it was time to learn.'

'Sure,' I said. 'This is just so you and I can get to learn about each other so we'll get along better, right?'

He nodded.

'But a date is a bit more, you know, romantic,' I said. 'That's not what this is.'

He looked surprised. 'But not always, surely,' he said. 'Don't people go on dates just to have fun?'

'Yeah, that too.'

'You said "too", which implies there's always a romantic element.' Now he looked troubled.

'Usually,' I said, then quickly added, 'but not in our case. I was just explaining things to you.' It was kind of like talking to a very innocent twelve year old—no, make that a ten year old—who also happened to be over four thousand years old. I sometimes wondered if he'd been asleep most of that time.

Thankfully the bus came then, cutting short our conversation. Rion loved bus trips. He usually watched everyone and then bombarded me with a zillion questions afterwards, but this time he seemed all thoughtful and quiet. He hardly said a word, even when we got off the bus and headed to the bowling alley.

Once inside, though, the clatter of rolling balls, the buzz of people laughing and talking, and the piped in music seemed to shake him out of his trance.

His eyes lit up. 'This is ... cool,' he said.

For once he got the word right. Sort of. Except I wouldn't exactly call a bowling alley cool.

There were far more people than I'd expected, and even though there weren't many my age everyone looked like they were having fun. Maybe tonight wouldn't be so bad after all.

We got the Hot Dog Bonanza, which included two games of bowling, shoe rental, and a hotdog, chips and a drink. Seemed a pretty good deal to me, and I noticed Mr Clean and Green didn't comment on the unhealthy snacks.

We went to our alley and sat down to put on our bowling shoes, which of course smelled absolutely feral. I looked down the long alley with the ten pins lined up neatly at the end. Then I looked at the heavy bowling balls. How on earth was I going to manage to get one of those balls down the alley, let alone knock anything over?

Let's be honest, I wasn't exactly into sport. Partly because it bored me silly, and partly because I wasn't all that coordinated. I didn't mind a leisurely swim at the beach or the pool, but that was about it. I wondered what Rion would be like.

Of course he knew the rules of scoring and everything.

'I've spent some time researching this game,' he said, as he tied his shoelaces neatly and stood up. 'I'm reasonably confident about the scoring, and I've also researched a few techniques and tips on how to bowl. Shall we begin?'

'Sure, I'll go first,' I said, wanting to get it over with. I grabbed a ball that seemed to weigh a tonne, and walked to the top of the alley.

'Find your mark by using the arrows, not the pins,' he instructed. 'And because you're right handed, aim to the right of the middle arrow.'

I tried to follow his instructions. Yep, eyes on the arrow.

'Now swing your arm back and then forward. Make sure you only release the ball when your arm's all the way to the front. Remember to keep your eyes on the target. Seems quite simple, really.' Rion sat down again and folded his arms to watch me.

I did everything he said to do, or at least I thought I did. But maybe my arm just wasn't strong enough. Despite my best efforts, the ball kind of dropped from my grasp and rolled in a zigzag movement down the alley, stopping about three-quarters of the way down.

'Did you even listen to what I said?' Rion said.

I turned on my heel, annoyed with the ball but annoyed equally with him. 'It's not that easy, you know.'

My next ball was no better, ending up in the gutter.

Rion got up. 'Clearly I'll have to knock your ball out of the way.'

Clearly. I sat down to watch the master.

He looked very confident, I had to give him that. He walked up to the balls and lifted one, testing its weight in his hands. Then he took his position, with his legs slightly apart, his knees bent and his back tilted forward. Checking his grip on the ball, he swung his arm backward and then forward. The ball dropped and actually bounced before promptly rolling into the gutter.

'Bad luck,' I said. 'Did you keep your eye on the arrow?' I couldn't resist it.

He gave me a look of total surprise. 'I can't believe it. I did everything according to the instructions. What happened?'

I raised an eyebrow. 'Maybe it's not quite as easy as it seems on the internet.'

'Something must've been wrong with those instructions. But I looked at several websites.'

Even though he'd only been in human form for a short time, Rion loved computers and he especially loved the internet. He thought every word he read was absolutely true.

'Maybe we just need more practice,' I said.

He nodded doubtfully. 'Maybe.'

Maybe I should've said a *lot* of practice. After a few attempts we eventually got the ball to stay in the lane and actually travel all the way down to the pins.

When he knocked over a couple of pins, I got up and cheered. 'Good work!' I cried, putting my hand in the air. 'High five.' He just looked at my hand, puzzled. 'Come on, you do the same thing,' I said.

When he cautiously raised his hand, I grinned and slapped it with mine. 'That's what you do when you congratulate someone about something they've done well.'

Part of his mouth went up in a crooked smile.

By the end of the first game, neither or us had managed to do more than knock down a few pins. 'We should try for a strike,' I said casually, 'or even a spare.' Rion raised his eyebrows. 'Yeah, well, you're not the only one who can use the lingo,' I said, 'but next time remember, actions speak louder than words.'

Now Rion looked embarrassed, but I decided to let him off lightly. 'I think it's time for a snack,' I said.

Rion looked at the hotdog. 'I don't even want to think about what goes into this.'

'Then don't.' I took a bite of mine. 'Oh, that's sooo good.'

He took a cautious bite and smiled. 'It's not too bad, although I'm sure it's not good for me.'

'Rion, you think entirely too much.' I picked up a chip and dipped it into the tomato sauce.

He looked puzzled. 'But isn't that the whole point of life, to think?'

Boy, did he have a lot to learn. 'Sometimes it's good just to be.'

'Hmm, okay.' He took another bite. 'I think I can manage this.' And manage it he did. He finished his hotdog, ate more than half the chips and downed his Coke. Then he gave a little burp.

I giggled.

'What's so amusing?'

'You. You know, Rion, you're not so bad when you forget to think.'

'Is that a compliment?' He looked pleased.

'Absolutely. Now let's get stuck into this second game. I'm determined to get a strike and beat you.'

'We'll see about that.' Rion scrunched up his paper cup, aimed at the rubbish bin and threw it in perfectly.

'Show-off,' I said.

He grinned. 'Yes, absolutely.'

The second game was much better. I didn't get a strike, but I did get a spare. I did a little dance and gave a whoop. 'I am sooo going to beat you,' I said.

Rion's eyes crinkled up and he laughed. 'Is that all you've got?' He got up, took a ball, aimed and then bowled a perfect strike.

I couldn't help it. I jumped up and down, and then ran over and gave him a hug. 'Wow!' I said.

After a microsecond he hugged me back, and I have to admit it felt kind of good. For a moment it felt like Rion was a real person, and I'm sure it was because for once he seemed to think he was, too.

'That was so awesome,' I said. And then I took a step back.

Rion looked at me with shiny eyes. 'You think so? You don't mind that it was me rather than you?'

'Nah,' I said, 'we're a team. I'm just glad one of us got a strike.'

The rest of the game went quickly, and it was kind of fun because neither of us cared who won. Rion even stopped keeping score.

We returned our shoes and headed out the door.

'You know, I didn't think this would be that great a night,' I said, 'but I was wrong. I really had fun.'

'Me, too,' he said. 'I definitely think we improved.'

'Absolutely.'

'High five,' he said, lifting his hand.

Laughing, I met it.

The trip home was more relaxed than the trip there. We talked about bowling technique, and what we did wrong and how we could improve. Normally this kind of thing would so have bored me, but tonight it didn't seem so bad.

We got off the bus and walked the short distance home.

'Thanks for coming out with me tonight,' Rion said as we stopped at the front door. 'I enjoyed your company, Zoe.'

'Yeah, I liked being with you, too. It was kind of … nice.'

'Maybe we can do it again sometime,' he said, a little shyly I thought.

'I'd like that. It was a pretty good date.' I wasn't lying either.

'I've been researching a lot about dates lately.'

I smiled. 'Yeah, I know.' I looked down at the yellow flower pinned to my muddy-brown cardigan. I was warming to it.

'There's just one more custom I'd like to try.' I was surprised to see him looking a bit embarrassed. 'It was very inappropriate when Jas did it, but I can see that it might be more appropriate in the context of a date.'

Suddenly butterflies started knocking themselves out in my stomach. Surely he wasn't thinking what I was. No, of course not. 'Not quite following you here,' I said.

'Well, if you don't mind, I think we should … kiss. Just to get the whole dating experience. You did say there was a romantic element involved in dates.'

I wasn't quite sure, but standing under the light at the front door, I think I saw him blush. Me? Those butterflies were now turning somersaults.

'But … but you said … you know, host and all that … maybe not a good idea.' I was having trouble making complete sentences.

'You said one thing tonight that made sense,' he said.

'Just one?'

He smiled. 'But it was a very wise thing. You said that sometimes I think too much.'

'Oh,' I said softly. 'Okay.'

He leaned forward and for a moment everything seemed to stop—my breathing, my heart, and definitely my thinking. Then his lips, warm and beautiful, touched mine. I closed my eyes and felt the gentle pressure of his mouth against mine. I responded, just a little. Even if he wasn't human, I was.

For what seemed a long time, our lips moved together and we had what was just about a perfect kiss. Then he moved back. Wow. Who would have thought an alien could kiss like that. I took a deep breath. I needed it after that. I noticed he was breathing deeply, too.

'That was very … satisfactory,' he said.

'Yeah,' was all I could say.

'And you know another very interesting fact?'

'No idea.' I was wishing we could try this little experiment again.

'Because you were originally my host, I don't think we need to worry nearly so much about germs. We've probably built up an immunity to each other's systems that keeps us safe. Very reassuring, isn't it?'

This time I was at a total loss for words.

Chapter Seventeen

I got the typical Mum reaction when I said I was going to a family barbecue with Harry Crosby.

'Such a lovely boy,' she said. 'He's quite smart, too, isn't he? Eileen told me he got straight A's in everything but physical education last year.'

Harry's mum, Eileen, taught prep at the same school where my mum taught year six, and I'd known him ever since we were four and in the same daycare. Maybe that's why we were friends and I tried to stand up for him when others made fun of him. Although I had to admit that he was a natural target at high school. Harry was a klutz. He was really shy and a bit plump—not fat, like some kids said unkindly, and I'd noticed he had lost a little weight lately—but once you got past all that, he was okay.

I sort of got why he'd asked me out. He needed a date and I was the only girl he knew that he could ask. And because we'd known each other a long time he wasn't as awkward with me as he was with everyone else. So, like with Rion, this was just a friendship date. But unlike with Rion, there would be no kissing, ever.

Showered and dressed, I went into the bathroom to finish getting ready. I smoothed the creases out of my denim skirt and brushed my hair up into a ponytail. It made me look younger than usual, but as Harry looked about twelve or thirteen, even though he was eight and a half months older than me, I figured that was okay. I flicked on some lip gloss and I was done.

Rion was in his room doing his favourite thing—studying with his door open. I felt awkward and shy after last night, but not wanting to act weird I decided to go in and talk to him, reminding myself that he was just an annoying little soap bubble of an alien who happened to materialise as a guy. Okay, he could easily have been on the cover of a teen magazine, but that was beside the point. It was all just an illusion. When I thought about it like that, I was okay.

He was sitting at his desk, bent over a book, his dark hair falling over his face. I leaned against the door for a moment, watching him. He didn't even look up.

No doubt he was working out some complicated maths problem or science formula. Such a geek.

'Concentration, much,' I said at last, when it appeared he would never notice I was there.

He didn't even act surprised when he looked up. Had he known I was there and was just pretending to study?

'Good morning, Zoe,' he said.

'So, what theory are you reinventing now?' I went into his room and perched on the side of his bed.

He gave his crooked smile. 'I'm just doing the maths homework for Monday. Have you finished it yet?'

'Yeah, sure, I've also done all my English, history and science for the whole week, as well as knocked out a few assignments this morning.'

He looked surprised for a moment, but then he said, 'Sarcasm, right?'

'Oh my God, you're finally getting it.'

'So, have you done *any* homework this weekend?' I could hear the disapproval in his tone.

'What do you think?'

He looked at me and shook his head. 'Don't leave it till the last minute. If you need any help, just ask.' He turned back to his book.

'Yeah, I've heard you're really good at that, helping with homework and all.'

I think Rion actually blushed. Sometimes he was just too easy to tease.

I got up to look out the window in case Harry and his mum arrived. 'Anyway, I haven't got time to study. I'm going out,' I said.

He looked up again. 'Out? Where?'

'Harry Crosby invited me to a family barbecue. He should be here any minute to pick me up.'

I started to head out the door, feeling my mission had been accomplished. We had talked. Rion had been preachy and judgemental, and I had been sarcastic, so everything was back to normal, thank goodness.

'Wait,' Rion said.

I turned around to face him. 'What?'

'I'm guessing this gathering is more than a hundred metres away,' he said, frowning.

And then it hit me and I remembered. 'Oh my God, of course, it's that distance thing between us again. We can't be too far apart. What am I going to do? He'll be here any minute.'

I collapsed on the bed. How could I have forgotten such an important thing? I had no idea where Harry's cousin lived, but it would be at least several kilometres away, enough of a distance to make us both seriously sick—or worse, if it was even further away.

'Logically, you have only two choices. You either don't go or I'll have to come too,' Rion said.

'I'll have to cancel. I'll pretend to be sick or something.' It wouldn't be a total lie because I knew I'd definitely be sick if I went to that barbecue.

'I guess I could come with you. It's inconvenient because I was hoping to get a start on my history assignment today, but I can catch up tonight.' Rion closed his book.

'No, you can't come because it's a date,' I said, then added, 'sort of.'

'What, another one? You've actually got another date this weekend? I thought it was just a family barbecue.'

Even though it was a family thing, and a date in friendship terms only, I kind of found it insulting that he should act so surprised.

'Yeah, I date,' I said. 'I haven't got two heads, you know. Some people even find me attractive.' I wasn't going to say that the only two people I could put in that category were my parents. No boys. He didn't have to know that.

'With Harry Crosby?'

'Yeah, I already said that.'

'I know I suggested you consider him as a boyfriend, but I didn't think you'd take me so literally, or act on my advice so quickly. You don't usually listen to anything I say.' He sounded peeved.

'Sorry, third parent, I didn't know I needed your permission. But Mum's all for it, FYI.'

'FYI?' he said, looking puzzled.

I kept forgetting he wasn't normal. 'For your information.'

'Oh, an acronym, I see.'

'Yeah, that, and what I'm saying is that Mum approves of Harry.'

Rion's forehead crinkled up in a frown. 'Your mother is an exceedingly kind person, but she's not always as critical as she might be.'

Now he sounded even crankier, if that was possible. And it was the closest he'd ever come to criticising my parents, who he put right up there with Stephen Hawking and the cast from *Happy Days;* I still didn't understand why he totally loved that series.

'What's wrong with Harry? I thought you liked him.'

'He's a bright, if somewhat socially awkward boy, and although I initially thought he might right for you I've revised my opinion. I think you should wait until someone more suitable comes along. Perhaps in a year or two. Besides, there are so many inherent problems with this dating thing. We've discussed them before.'

Of course we had, and I knew dating would be tricky with Rion around, but I didn't want to go through the rest of high school like a nun. Rion's attitude was getting on my nerves.

'Don't be a pompous prat,' I said. 'We're going to have to try and find a solution because I'm not going through high school never dating again.'

I heard a car pull up outside. 'And we'd better find one quickly because Harry's just arrived.'

I wondered if I could fake a sudden attack of stomach cramp or a splitting headache. It would totally hurt Harry, who would suspect I was putting it on and didn't want to go. And there was the Mum factor. I hadn't shown the slightest sign of sickness when I was talking to her ten minutes ago. She wouldn't be happy with me. But I knew I had no other choice.

Hearing the knock on the door, I headed downstairs to face Harry. I opened the door to see him looking all eager and happy. He was dressed in long khaki shorts and a new white T-shirt. His hair had gel in it and was kind of spiky. Sigh. This was Harry making a big effort. And now I was about to tell him I couldn't go.

'Hi Zoe, you look nice,' he said, beaming at me.

'Thanks. You look good, too. Come in,' I said, opening the door wider.

'Hello, Harry, how are you?' Mum drifted through the hall carrying a basket of clean laundry.

'Good thanks, Mrs Brennan.'

'Zoe's been so looking forward to this barbecue,' she said. 'Well, I won't keep you as I know your mum's waiting in the car. Say hello from me. Have a good time, you two.' She gave us a wave and headed up the stairs with the laundry.

Gee, thanks Mum, I thought. She'd only made it harder for me to tell Harry I couldn't go.

'I'm sorry, but I've got some bad news,' I said, feeling like the biggest jerk in the universe.

Just at that moment Rion came down the stairs, taking them two at a time. He was wearing a clean shirt and had changed from his daggy shorts into jeans.

'Hi Harry,' he said. 'What Zoe's trying to say is that I'm coming to the barbecue, too. I hope that's okay.'

Harry looked totally surprised and not altogether pleased. But he was polite, so all he said was, 'Oh, I hadn't realised, but of course you're welcome.'

I waited for Rion to give an explanation of why he was going to crash our date. Surely someone as smart as him could come up with something. But he didn't seem to feel any explanation was necessary. This alien really didn't get things sometimes.

So I said, 'Sorry, Harry, I should've let you know earlier. Rion hasn't had much of a chance to socialise or get out much since he's been here. Mum and Dad thought it might be a good idea for him to meet a few people. You don't mind, do you?'

It was the best I could come up with on such short notice. Mum and Dad would never know I'd blamed them for this. I gave Harry my best smile.

Of course he smiled back. 'Sure, no worries.' He turned to Rion. 'All my family will be there, plus my cousin, who's around our age. So there'll be lots of people to meet and they're not totally horrible.' He gave an awkward little laugh.

'I look forward to meeting them,' Rion said.

I followed them both out the door. I just wanted this day to come to an end. I had an uneasy feeling that things were not going to get better. In fact, they could get a whole lot worse. Great.

Chapter Eighteen

Everyone made Rion feel welcome, of course. Harry's family were like that. I wondered if Mum had told Mrs Crosby about Rion's 'unfortunate' home circumstances, because Harry's mum was especially kind to him.

'I'm so glad you could join us, Rion,' she said. 'Harry's cousins will be delighted to meet you.'

And that was very true, especially in the case of Mary-Jo, the girl who was turning eighteen. It didn't matter that Rion was supposedly two years younger; Mary-Jo made sure she was in charge of entertaining him. She would have rivalled Jas in the attention she gave him. And it didn't hurt that he only had to smile to make hearts flutter. He was very polite, and almost charming, for him anyway, and everyone loved him.

Harry and I were hardly even noticed, but that was good. It took the pressure off. The last thing I wanted was to be the centre of attention, especially since I knew this was the first time Harry had brought a girl anywhere. He gave me a diet Coke and we sat down near the pool. Being winter, no one was swimming, which was great because we were away from everyone else and any questions that might come my way once the fascination with Rion was over.

The pool gate banged and a couple of the younger cousins raced in, followed by a very large golden Labrador dog.

'Hey, no running through here,' Harry reminded them. 'And you know you're not supposed to let the dog in, either.'

The two little kids with red hair and freckles stopped to look at us. One of them smirked and said, 'Hey, Harry, is that your girlfriend?'

'Yeah, are you gonna kiss her?' the other one said.

Sometimes I'm really glad I don't have any little brothers or sisters.

Aside from blushing, Harry ignored them. 'Will you guys get Rusty out of here?' he said. 'You know how he always jumps—'

Too late. Even as he spoke, the hyper dog jumped in the pool and practically caused a tsunami. I was sitting closest to the pool and a wall of water washed over me, soaking my clothes and my hair. The can of Coke slipped from my hands and fell on the tiles, mixing with the water that was now everywhere. The redheaded cousins were totally dry, and Harry had only caught a few sprinkles of water on his T-shirt. Meanwhile, Rusty was having a great time swimming to the other end of the pool.

'Oh no.' Harry jumped up and futilely tried to brush the water off my skirt. 'Are you okay?'

I rose from the deck chair and tried to shake off some of the water. 'I'm fine,' I said, but I was moving back towards the edge of the pool and my foot slipped. I swayed, lost my balance and fell into the water, making an even bigger splash than Rusty.

I flailed about for a few seconds and then stood up. The water was just above my waist. OMG, that water was cold. Could this day get any worse, I asked myself? I shouldn't have asked.

Harry looked at me horror-struck for a moment, and then he bent down and held out a hand. 'Zoe, are you okay?' he asked for a second time. 'Here, let me help you.'

'I'm fine,' I said again. I clambered out of the pool, ignoring Harry's hand. Knowing my luck, I'd probably only end up dragging him in, too.

He looked at the two round-eyed cousins. 'See what you've done? Get that dog out of here *now*.'

One of the kids rushed to pull the ecstatic dog out of the pool.

The other one said, 'Sorry.'

Of course Rusty shook himself when he was out of the pool, sending another shower of water our way. What did it matter? I was already soaked through.

The boys dragged the dog out of the pool area while Harry glared at them. 'Just wait till I tell Aunt Meg,' he said.

'We said sorry,' the taller one said, and then they disappeared as fast as they could.

'Those little monsters,' Harry said. 'I'm so sorry, Zoe. They know better than to let the dog in the pool area. Rusty's still only a pup and hasn't learned how to be obedient yet. He just loves water.'

'Yeah, I got that,' I said. 'Don't worry, it's no big deal, and it wasn't the kids' fault I fell into the water. It was an accident. Me and my klutzy actions.' I tried to smile. Large drops from my wet ponytail trailed down my back. I didn't even want to think about what I looked like.

'I'll get you a towel, and maybe Mary-Jo has some spare things she can lend you.'

'I'll be fine with a towel,' I said.

But of course the Crosby family wouldn't let me away with that.

'Oh, you poor dear, what happened?' Eileen Crosby said as we approached the back deck where most of the guests were sitting. I was dripping water all over the deck, leaving puddles behind me.

'Let me guess,' said Harry's Aunt Meg, who was also Mary-Jo's mum. 'It was Rusty.'

'Who let him in the pool area?' one of the uncles asked.

'I just bet it was Ethan and Josh,' Mary-Jo said.

Naturally the boys were nowhere in sight.

'I'll deal with them later,' Aunt Meg said in an ominous tone. 'Now, dear, you come with me and we'll get you into something warm and dry.'

'I'm fine,' I said for the umpteenth time. I tried to explain that I had fallen into the water all by myself, but I didn't get a chance to get the words out.

'Nonsense,' she said firmly. 'You're already starting to shiver.'

Before I could say another word, she was leading me into the house. I looked back and caught Rion's eye. His mouth was turned up at the corners, and I could have sworn he was trying not to laugh. In some ways he wasn't much better than those redheaded kids.

Despite my protests, a few minutes later I was wearing one of Mary-Jo's T-shirts, which was several sizes too big, and a pair of track pants that would've fallen down if I hadn't pulled in the drawstring tightly. My wet hair was wrapped in a towel. What an attractive look. Just as well I didn't care, not much anyway.

I went back out to sit on the deck with all the aunts and the gazillion cousins. Now I was the centre of attention. Oh joy. At least the uncles were drinking beer around the barbecue and mostly ignored us, thank goodness.

'Zoe, you're in some of Harry's classes at school, aren't you?' said another of the aunts.

'Harry and Zoe have known each other for years,' said Eileen, Harry's mum. 'They went to kindy together.'

I felt the gaze of at least six pairs of eyes. I readied myself for the second tsunami, but this time of questions rather than water.

'How sweet,' the aunt said. 'Now that I think of it, I'm sure I've heard Harry mention you before.'

'Yes, me too,' said another aunt or friend or someone old, smiley and nosy. 'Didn't you two go to the same school camp together?'

Along with the rest of our grade, I thought, but whatever. I just smiled.

'Harry, you and Zoe will have to come to little Beth's christening next month. Oh, and you too Rion if you're free,' said another aunt who was dangling a fat baby on her knee.

Harry looked just as embarrassed as me.

Aunt Meg came to the rescue. 'Why don't you get Zoe another drink, Harry? And pass her the sausage rolls, Izzy. The poor girl must be starving after that ordeal. I hope someone tied up that dog.' Then she spied the two young boys, who were trying hard not to be noticed as they slid a bowl of potato chips from one of the side tables. 'Ethan and Josh, come here now.'

Looking like they'd rather be anywhere else, the boys put down the bowl and reluctantly came forward.

'How many times have I told you not to let that dog into the pool area?' She fixed them with a look that only mums can do.

'Lots,' they said in unison.

'You're just lucky it's your sister's birthday or else you'd both be on your way to your room now. Apologise to poor Zoe.'

'That's okay, they already did,' I said. I was actually starting to feel sorry for them. But they apologised again anyway. I was beginning to suspect that Aunt Meg was not a person to cross.

'Now go and collect the empty glasses and bring them into the kitchen,' she told them. 'You can consider the computer off limits for the rest of the day.'

'Aw, Mum,' they said in protest.

'Go. Now.'

They disappeared quickly.

Making my own escape, I moved to the back of the deck where Mary-Jo was sitting next to Rion and drinking champagne, which she could have now because she was an adult, technically speaking. She had one elbow on the arm of his chair.

'I'm so glad Zoe brought you, Rion,' I heard her say as I approached. 'I thought this family thing for my birthday would be so boring, but hey, the company's not so bad after all.' She gave him a wide smile.

Could she have been any more obvious?

'I went out to the city with my friends on Friday night and I was sooo hungover the next day.' She giggled. 'Do you want a sip?' she said, offering Rion her champagne. 'Or better still, a whole glass? I could put it in a plastic cup and no one would know. Not that Uncle Bob or Uncle Aaron would care, but Mum and Aunt Eileen are, you know, a bit strict. Out of the ark, really. And anyway, you could easily pass for eighteen, nineteen, even twenty.'

Before Rion could answer, I said, 'Hey, how's it going?'

'Oh Zoe, there you are,' Mary-Jo said, as if I hadn't been standing there for a couple of minutes. 'You poor thing, how are you feeling now?'

'I'm okay. Thanks for the loan of the clothes.'

'No worries,' she said. 'Hey, you and Harry are a cute couple. You really suit each other.' I knew she was just trying to be nice, but more and more I wished I hadn't come to this barbecue.

'We're just friends,' I said.

Rion looked at me with his dark brown eyes and an unreadable expression.

'Of course. Oh, there he is now. Harry, she's over here,' Mary-Jo called. 'Rion, you just have to see what my parents got me for my birthday. It's a MacBook Pro. So cool. Didn't you say you were into computers? Come on and I'll show you.'

She had said the one thing that was guaranteed to catch his interest. He got up and followed her into the house.

The food was being put out, so Harry and I walked over and filled plates.

'Let's sit down by the mango tree,' Harry said. 'Uncle Brian put a seat there, and it's nice and warm so you might dry off quicker.'

'Sure,' I said, though I'd been perfectly happy on the deck.

The mango tree was around the side of the house, away from the prying eyes of the rest of the party. I wondered, just for a fleeting moment, about Harry's motivation. But hey, I reminded myself, this was Harry, my kindy buddy, my lab partner, the guy who let me copy his homework.

I sat down and took off the hideous towel, put it on the back of the seat and shook my damp hair. Harry sat beside me and we balanced out plates on our knees.

'You've been really cool about everything, Zoe,' Harry said, tucking into a sausage. 'You know, coming here today and being such a good sport about getting soaked. Thanks for that.'

I looked down. My sausage had dripped sauce onto Mary-Jo's clean white T-shirt. Of course. 'That's okay, Harry. Thanks for asking me.' I knew how to be polite, even if I had to force the words out a bit.

Then his hand sneaked out and covered mine. I felt the pressure of his warm fingers. Oh no.

'I really like you, Zoe. And I was wondering if …'

His face came closer to mine and then I suddenly realised what he was going to do. I turned my face just in time, and his lips grazed my cheek. He sat back looking all red and awkward.

I decided to cut in before he could say anything that would embarrass us both even more. 'I like you too, Harry. You're a really good friend. Let's keep it that way.' I smiled at him but I could see that I had upset him.

I slipped my hand away from his and got up just as Rion came around the corner. He looked at us then quirked an eyebrow at me. Jeez, had he seen?

All he said was, 'They're going to bring out the cake for Mary-Jo now.'

I moved away from both him and Harry. I needed some space.

We went back up to the deck where everyone, even the uncles, had gathered.

'Okay everyone,' Mary-Jo's mum called out, 'we're about to bring in the birthday cake.'

Mary-Jo was pushed toward the table. She was trying to look bored, but I could see that she was kind of pleased. Her mum came out onto the deck carefully carrying a large birthday cake, all eighteen of its candles flickering in the late afternoon breeze, and everyone started to sing 'Happy Birthday'.

I moved aside to make way for the cake and as I did so my foot slipped on a puddle of water, probably left behind from my dip in the pool. My shoes were still drying in the sun, and my feet were bare. One foot slipped and I started to fall. It was like seeing something in slow motion in a dream—you know what's going to happen, but you can't do anything to stop it.

I fell against Mary-Jo's mum and the birthday cake (a double-layer black forest cake with glacé cherries, cream, thick chocolate frosting and eighteen candles) went crashing to the deck. For a microsecond there was complete silence. To me it felt like the universe had stood still. Then there was a collective intake of breath.

Cake, frosting and cherries were splattered on the deck like a scene from one of those violent movies when someone has just copped it bad. I usually turn my head when that happens on the screen, but in this case all I could do was stare at the damage in horrified fascination, taking in every gory detail around me as I sat on the floor. At least the candles had spluttered out—one small mercy—so nothing caught on fire.

Okay, here's the thing. Harry's family is super-nice and they would never deliberately make anyone feel badly about anything, especially if it wasn't their fault. But there are just some days when you know you shouldn't get out of bed. Today was one of them.

Pandemonium broke out. Mary-Jo squealed, one of the uncles swore (softly) and the red-haired terrors broke out in giggles. Then Rusty, who had somehow gotten untied, burst onto the scene, weaving through legs and heading straight for the cake. He started to eat it up as if he hadn't been fed in a week.

Recovering from her shock, Aunt Meg burst into action. She grabbed Rusty's collar with one hand and started dragging him away from the mess, while her other hand reached out to me. 'Are you all right, Zoe?'

Somehow I managed to say, 'Yes. I'm so sorry. I slipped on the wet deck.' I looked over at Mary-Jo and repeated, 'I'm really sorry, Mary-Jo.'

I could see that Mary-Jo was making a visible effort not to be upset. 'That's okay. Not your fault.'

'Harry, tie up the dog,' Aunt Meg said. 'Would everyone mind going into the lounge room while we clean this up? Eileen, there's some ice cream and fruit in the fridge. We can have that. Mary-Jo, you organise the tea and coffee.'

Everyone moved away to do exactly what she said. I suspected Aunt Meg would have made a terrific general or something; she was so calm and organised in a crisis. I tried to help her clean up the mess, but she stopped me.

'Why don't you go and get cleaned up, Zoe?' she said. 'I put your clothes in the dryer, and they should be dry by now.'

'But I want to help you.'

'Of course not, you're our guest. Don't you worry about a thing,' she said. 'It's not your fault you slipped. I should have wiped up the water on the deck, but I didn't see it. That was very careless of me. Off you go now and get dressed.'

And like everyone else, I did exactly what she said.

Although everyone made an effort, and jokes were even made about how it was the best birthday Rusty had ever had, things kind of fizzled out after that. It wasn't too much later that Harry's mum asked us if we were ready to go home.

I had been ready before I even got here.

Everyone was very quiet on the drive home, and it was a relief to say goodbye. Harry had been acting all awkward ever since the kiss incident, and I wondered if things would ever be the same between us. I couldn't wait to go up to my room and forget this day had ever happened.

'Hi, you two,' Mum called as she looked up from her newspaper. 'How'd the barbecue go?'

Rion answered. 'I can honestly say it was the most interesting party I've ever been to. You might even say it was a crashing success.' He looked at me and smiled.

So now he had decided to learn how to make a joke.

'I'm going upstairs to study,' I said, leaving both of them open mouthed. Anything was better than 'social interaction' at the moment.

Chapter Nineteen

I so wanted to stay home on Monday. I was totally spent and I really didn't want to face Harry today, after what had happened at the party. Also, I knew Jas and the girls would give me the third degree about my date with Rion on the weekend. It would be great to stay home and maybe watch Netflix, eat junk food and try to forget that everything in my life was going south at the moment.

But that was never going to happen. Mum, being a schoolteacher and a total nerd, would never let me have days off school unless I was absolutely dying. Sadly, I looked far from that, even though I felt it. So I dragged myself out of bed and got ready for school.

Rion seemed unusually quiet and thoughtful when I went down for breakfast. For once he actually had a coffee instead of his usual organic green tea and orange juice.

And he never even touched his muesli. Mum and Dad had already left for work so we had the kitchen to ourselves.

'What's up?' I said at last to break the silence.

He looked at me for a moment and then said, 'Do you like Harry?'

That was the last thing I expected him to say. 'Are you serious?' I put down my cup.

'I think it's a reasonable question. After all, you agreed to go on a date with him and he does seem to like you.'

Maybe he'd seen Harry's disastrous attempt to kiss me. I rushed to reassure him, in case he had the wrong idea. 'Harry and I have known each other for, like, forever. We played in the same sandpit together when we were four. We went to the same primary school and now we're at the same high school. He's like a brother, that's all. I only went out with him because he needed a date and I kind of felt sorry for him. And let's not get carried away with this date thing. After all, I went out with you and we both know that meant absolutely nothing.'

I sat back in my chair and took another sip of coffee.

Rion eyes flickered and I almost imagined I saw something that looked like emotion in them. But I was obviously mistaken. My alien didn't believe in emotions. He'd told me that often enough.

'Good to know, although I could see that he clearly had feelings for you, Zoe, and I don't think as a sibling,' Rion said. 'You might not want to give him any encouragement.'

'Not that it's any of your business,' I said, 'but I don't intend to. Anyway, that's enough about Harry. Let's get going. We've missed the bus, but we can still make it on time if we walk, as long as we leave now.'

I couldn't have said anything to make him move faster. If there was one thing Rion hated, it was being late for school. But I wondered why he had asked me such a weird question.

School was just about as bad as I expected. Harry was awkward. I mean he usually was with other people, but not with me. Now he was being ultra polite and avoiding eye contact. He knew now that any feelings I had for him were the friend type and not the boyfriend type. I really wished he felt the same way because a) I didn't want him to feel hurt, and b) I didn't want to lose the real friendship we'd had for so many years.

Life was just too complicated at times.

And then Jas cornered me in the girls' loo. 'So, how did things go with you and Rion on Saturday night?' she asked as I was washing my hands at the sink. She took out her brush and began to run it through her already perfect hair.

'Fine,' I said.

I dried my hands with a paper towel and tried to get away, but I was too slow. As I turned toward the door she moved in front of me. She stood with her hand on hip, blocking my escape.

'What did you guys do?' There was a smile on her face but calculation in her eyes.

That was a question I didn't want to answer because I knew how lame it would sound. But I had no choice. 'We went bowling.'

Jas's face cracked into a smile and she laughed. 'How cute. That's what you'd take a little sister to or something. I mean, bowling? It's not like a real date, is it?'

I could have wiped the smile right off her face by saying that Rion and I had kissed. But I didn't want to share that information with her. I knew the knives would come out for sure, and believe me, Jas's knives were sharp. I'd seen her other victims. Up to now I hadn't been important enough to be one of them.

'It was okay, Jas. We had fun. See you later.' I pushed past her and out the door. As I walked down the corridor I knew I hadn't heard the last of it.

And I hadn't. At lunchtime I was tempted to sit away from her group, but it would have looked like I had something to hide, and then I'd be a target until they found out what it was. So I sat down as usual.

Rion was in the lab. He'd managed to get a little part-time work helping and cleaning up in the lab. He was such a nerd and the science teachers loved him, so that had helped. The job also gave him a little money, which he desperately needed because he hated taking anything from my parents. I supposed that showed character or something noble like that. Anyway, it meant he either wouldn't be joining the group for lunch, or he would be late and just scoff down his sandwich before the bell.

Jas was playing with her fork in a salad she probably wouldn't eat. 'Hey, guys,' she said, 'you'll never guess where Rion and Zoe went on their date on Saturday night. Tell them, Zoe,' She looked at me pointedly.

'Why don't you tell them, Jas, since you seem so interested and all,' I said.

She didn't need a second invite. 'They went bowling,' she said, pausing for dramatic effect.

She got the reaction she wanted. There were smirks from the boys, and eye rolls and looks from the girls. Chelsea smothered a giggle.

Whatever had made me think these people were my friends? I looked over at my old group, where Harry and the others were sitting. They weren't the cool kids, but they weren't unkind either. But Harry was ignoring me, and going over to sit with them would present a whole lot of other problems.

I turned back and looked at the many pairs of mocking eyes, wishing that Rion were here. I knew they wouldn't dare act this way if he were. Okay, time to sort them out.

'Yeah, we went bowling,' I said. 'It was really cool. We had heaps of fun and we might even go again.'

'But that's not really a date, is it? Seriously, bowling? I mean, isn't that what old people, little kids and losers do, bowl? No offence.' Jas twirled her hair in one hand and looked at me with spiteful eyes. 'But I guess Rion was just taking you out because he felt he had to. Maybe your parents asked him to or something.'

I took a deep breath before I said something I really regretted. I needed to turn on the smarts. I couldn't let Jas have this one. I mentally counted to ten.

'Soz, Jas,' I said, 'I know you had to ask, practically beg, Rion to help you with your homework. FYI, he was kind of embarrassed about that. But he did actually ask me out and he was the one who suggested bowling. He thought it would be really cool, and it was. As a matter of fact, it ended pretty well, too.' I put on my most mysterious and smug smile. Let them think whatever they liked. And going by the looks on their faces, they were thinking plenty.

Jas turned an interesting shade of red. It looked like she was about to explode. But before she could say anything, Rion himself came strolling over.

'Hi, guys,' he said.

He was really getting the lingo now. But then he was a quick learner.

Then I did something I knew I would probably regret, but I never gave myself time to think about it. I stood up, grabbed Rion by the shirt collar and planted a kiss right on those warm, McDreamy lips. I think he might have, just a bit, returned the pressure. Then I let him go.

'Great to see you, babe, I missed you,' I said.

Okay, if I thought knocking over the birthday cake at the barbecue made an impact surprise it was nothing compared to that kiss. Shock and awe might be a better term, and that included Rion. He stepped back and his eyes widened. I wished I had that mind-meld thingy going on right then because I would've sent a telepathic message: *Don't mess this up for me, Rion. Play along.*

But I wondered if he could read my mind anyway because, after a microsecond, he gave that crooked smile and said, 'I missed you too, babe.' Then he pulled me close and whispered in my ear, 'You'd better have a good explanation for this.'

'Oh, look at the time,' Jas said. 'I've got a dozen things to do before class. Chad, honey, can you help me out, I've got a stack of things to pick up at the library. I might need an extra pair of hands.'

Chad, looking like he'd just won Gold Lotto, said, 'Sure thing, Jas.'

'Great. Let's go.'

Jas took his hand and pulled him away. Usually that would be a signal for the group to disperse, but not today. All the attention was directed at Rion and me as everyone waited to see what would happen next.

'Rion, I was just telling everyone what fun we had at bowling,' I said, using my best girly voice.

Rion gave me a look. 'Yes, it was quite entertaining, Zoe.'

Chelsea was looking at me through narrowed eyes, and I knew she would report everything that was said. 'So,' she said, 'are you two going out now?'

I hesitated. If I said yes that would make life way too complicated, and it would mean the end of any possible real dating for me in the future. If I said no then everyone would wonder what was going on and how sincere our little act was.

I looked at Rion and signalled with my eyes: *Help!* Thank God he could read me well.

'Zoe and I want to get to know each other better before we make any commitment,' he said, then flashed a smile that seemed to say a lot more than his words. I thought it was a fairly perfect answer.

Before anyone could say anything else, the bell rang.

'We really need to get to history,' Rion said, taking my hand and pulling me along. 'See you guys later.' As soon as we got out of earshot, he dropped my hand. 'So, would you like to tell me what that was all about?'

'I thought we had to get to history class on time. We don't want to be late.' I wasn't eager to have this conversation.

'Since when has that ever bothered you? Besides, we have exactly four minutes and twenty-five seconds before the final bell, plenty of time for you to explain things. What happened back there?'

I sighed. 'Jas was making fun of the fact that we went bowling. She said it was a place you'd take your little sister and not a real date, and of course the others were following her lead. I just wanted to shut them up. Sorry for putting you on the spot like that. And thanks for playing along with it.'

'So they were, in effect, bullying you?' A frown came over his face.

'I don't think it was as bad as that. It's just the way they are.'

'You know, Zoe, I think you could've chosen better friends. That group seems to demonstrate the worst traits in human beings—you know, the herd instinct and the propensity to target the weak.'

'Sometimes they're okay.' I didn't know why I was defending them. I was beginning to think Rion had a point.

'I differ on that opinion. I can see, though, that we'll have to talk about this further. I anticipated that there might be some problems with our relationship, but I hadn't expected them to develop quite so quickly. We'll talk about it after school. Now we really do have to get to class.'

I wasn't very comfortable with how this conversation was going. I was starting to feel like a fool for having kissed Rion and trying to save face with people who I was beginning to realise weren't worth the effort.

For once I was actually glad to get to class.

It was a long day, and more than once I wished I hadn't kissed Rion. Jas totally ignored me, and now I felt weird with Rion *and* Harry. Of course Rion acted normally, for him at least, and was super-attentive in class and ignoring everyone but the teacher. If I hadn't known him better I would've said he was a total suck-up. But, sadly, I knew he was just a nerd who loved learning. Never mind that he knew more than the teachers anyway.

But now we had kissed twice, and even though I knew it meant absolutely nothing, especially on his part, it had kind of felt nice. And that was the weird part. Rion wasn't even real, at least not in any human sense. And he was way too old for me. Ha, ha, joke. He was too old even for my great-great-great-grandmother, whoever she was.

The problem was that he'd chosen to package himself as the most beautiful sixteen-year-old boy possible. I wished he'd gone for something slightly less awesome. I mean, other than his looks, we had no connection at all. Okay, we did get on all right when we went bowling. And sometimes I could bear to talk to him when he wasn't showing off or being bossy, but other than that, zilch.

After school we met outside the gate.

'Bus or walk?' he asked, shaking his head to get his fringe out of his eyes. Some boys did that for effect, but Rion did it so he could see.

223

'Walk.' I started walking down the street. Anything that avoided people was my preferred option this afternoon.

He swung into step beside me. For a few minutes neither of us said anything. And that suited me, too. As far as I was concerned, what had happened at lunchtime was over, history, never to be repeated again.

Rion, however, had other ideas. 'We need to talk,' he said, as we turned the corner and were out of earshot and sight of anyone else.

'Yeah, now you mention it, I could really do with some help on that history assignment,' I said, hoping to deflect his attention from anything personal.

'You're good in history. You'll be fine,' he said, shifting his books to his other arm and placing a hand on my shoulder. He stopped and turned me to face him. 'Why did you kiss me, Zoe, in front of your group?'

'You know why. I told you. They were putting me down and I wanted to show them I wasn't a loser. Stupid move, I know. Sorry if it embarrassed you.' It annoyed me that even feeling his hand on my shoulder felt nice, reassuring.

He shook his head impatiently. 'It didn't embarrass me. It surprised me. I understand what you were trying to do, but you could've chosen something less dramatic. I mean, you could've just said that you missed me without that kiss, or even just held my hand. But kissing me like that … you did it like you meant it. Which leads me to think you really wanted to. Are you attracted to me, Zoe?'

'What? No! Eeuw! How could you think such a thing?' I took a step back and his hand slipped off my shoulder. 'It was an act. Totally and completely.'

Rion put his head to one side and looked at me. 'No, not totally and not completely,' he said. 'I've had three kisses with humans now, which, by the way, has been fascinating and informative in terms of my research on human behaviour. The first one with Jas was interesting because it was a novel experience, but that was it. The second one, with you on Saturday night, was actually mildly enjoyable, to my surprise. It gave me a glimpse of what these human emotions are all about. But the one today was different again. There was increased pressure on the lips, mainly from you, I might add. It was definitely enjoyable again, and this time even somewhat exciting. I believe I had an elevated pulse rate and my breathing was shallow afterwards. You also had the same reaction, I observed.'

I stood there speechless, but only for a moment. Then I exploded. 'I did *not*. I was just angry at those jerks I call friends. And damn it, Rion, do you have to analyse *everything*, even kissing? What kind of freak are you? And as if I'd enjoy kissing someone who was a total alien weirdo.'

Okay, maybe I shouldn't have said those two last sentences. But sometimes he drove me to say and do things I wouldn't normally do.

His lips made a straight line and his eyes darkened. Maybe aliens did feel something after all. 'You're right,' he said. 'I'm not human, and this state of being is not normal for me. Now I truly understand why our species has been so reluctant to take human form. It was never a wise idea, despite the extensive research that could have been done. Human beings are too faulty, and their emotions make everything ... messy. I'll endeavour to contact my people again. I've tried to make a mental connection with my supervisor, but he has several hundred others of my kind to oversee so he might not respond for a while. I'll try again. My unique situation may cause him to respond more quickly than usual.' He turned away from me and started to walk again.

That little speech gave me some hope. Maybe we wouldn't have to wait years after all. I rushed to catch up with him. 'So, if he contacts you what will happen?'

'I'm hoping he'll return me to my natural state,' Rion said, not looking at me.

I thought about it for a moment. 'Does that mean ... we'll still be connected?' I wasn't sure how I felt about that.

'I honestly don't know. I hope not. I don't think that would be wise, all things considered. I really would prefer to return to the mothercloud and wait for a more suitable host.'

His long legs were taking large strides and I had to rush to keep up. Usually he adapted his pace to mine, but today he looked like he was in training for speed walking in the Olympics.

'So we wouldn't, like, know each other any more?' I asked.

'Obviously I'll remember the connection because I have a perfect memory, but you might choose to forget. However, if you mean that we'll have no contact with each other again, yes, that's an accurate assumption.'

The thought of never talking to Rion again, or arguing with him, or hearing one of his many hundreds of lectures about everything under the sun made me feel kind of sad. Yes, he was annoying at times, and yes, at the beginning I wanted nothing more than to be rid of him. But I knew him now. He was real to me.

'I wouldn't choose to forget you, Rion,' I said, feeling a lump in my throat.

He didn't answer me. We turned down our street.

'Can you slow down a bit?' I said. 'Struggling to keep up here.'

'Oh,' he said, slowing his pace just a little, 'I forgot you weren't very fit.'

'I'm perfectly fit,' I snapped. 'You happen to be a lot taller than me so you can walk faster. I think we should talk some more about this.'

He slowed down a bit more. 'I don't think there's much else to say, Zoe. I can see my presence is very uncomfortable for you and has complicated your life. I will endeavour, as I said, to remove my freaky, weirdo alien self as soon as I can.'

'Jeez, Rion, don't be so sensitive. I'm sorry I said those things.'

'But from your point of view, that observation is correct.' He stared straight ahead, not making eye contact. Obviously still upset.

'But you're also my friend, and if you went away I would miss you.' I took a deep breath. I realised it was true.

He stopped again. This time he looked at me. 'But I'm not at all like you. You argue with me and rarely listen to my advice. It doesn't seem logical that you consider me a friend.'

'We also have fun sometimes, like when we went bowling. And you stuck up for me and didn't give me away to my group when I kissed you today. And you wouldn't even have a human form at all if you hadn't tried to help me. In many ways you've been a much better friend to me than my so-called "friends" in the group.'

I could see the beginnings of his crooked smile. 'Perhaps you're right. They're not very nice to you. You should change groups.'

'Yes, I was thinking that,' I said. 'I might go back to Harry's group—if they'll have me.'

'I'm sure Harry would.'

'Seriously, we are just friends.'

'Like you and me?'

'Yeah, I guess so, but …' I looked at him sideways. 'I've never kissed Harry. And you're right, I did have an elevated pulse thingy when we kissed.' Hard to admit, but it was true. Perhaps that was why I reacted the way I did.

'Oh.' He processed that for a moment. And then he added, 'So, you would miss me?'

'Absolutely. I mean who else is going to tell me about the nutritional value of Coco Pops?'

'Coco Pops have no nutritional value, you know that,' he said in his nearly normal condescending voice.

'I do now.' I gave him a cheeky grin. 'What would I do without you?'

'I have no doubt you'd go on in your usual haphazard way, putting your health and your education at serious risk. In other words, you would just be a normal teenager.'

'Not quite normal, Rion.' My books were getting heavy and I shifted them to my other arm.

'What do you mean?'

'Because now that I've met you I can never be quite the same again.' And that was true. I mean, how many people have met an alien, let alone become friends with them?

He took my books and added them to his own. 'I guess that's also accurate for me, too. I'll never be the same again, either. I've never met a human quite like you, Zoe. You've opened my eyes to some unique experiences. I've learned more from you in a few weeks than I have in decades with my other hosts.'

I think, though I wasn't sure, that my alien had just given me a compliment. After all, he did place a high value on learning.

We started to walk again. 'So, friends, then?'

'Friends,' he said, matching his stride to mine this time.

Chapter Twenty

'You've got to be joking. There's no way I'm going to the State Library on my birthday,' I said.

For Rion, going to the State Library would be equivalent of receiving the best birthday and Christmas gifts ever for the next decade or so. He really thought he'd come up with a great idea.

'But we could also do some research for our history assignment on the federation of Australia. And ...' his eyes sparkled as if he was about to give me tickets to a Katie Perry concert or something, 'we could also go to the science museum, which is only a three and a half minute walk away, probably four minutes for you as you do walk a bit slowly.'

'Yay. And while we're at it why don't we do the art gallery as well? We could follow it up with an exciting cup of herbal tea.'

His face lit up even more, if that was possible. 'What an excellent suggestion.' He stopped and looked at me more closely. 'But you don't seem very pleased, Zoe. In fact, your voice sounds flat. Perhaps I'm not as good at reading human reactions as I thought, but your words don't correspond to either your facial or vocal signals.'

'Ya think?' I said, and flopped down on the chair beside his desk. Sometimes it was exhausting interacting with my alien.

'Oh, I see. Sarcasm again.' He sat down on the bed opposite me. 'I'm still learning about that.'

'Give the man a prize.'

I knew he was only trying to be helpful. I would be sixteen in two weeks and it was a milestone birthday I'd been looking forward to for ages. In fact, I'd hoped to have a party with all my cool new friends. For a micro-minute or two I'd even imagined Chad Everett playing a major role in the celebrations as my boyfriend. But that was all ancient history now. Chad and Jas were a thing now, although she still flirted with Rion occasionally, mainly out of habit, I think. Basically, Jas flirted with any male under thirty. She ignored me, of course, except to throw a barbed comment my way, but only a couple of times a day.

I didn't sit with Jas and her group at lunchtime anymore. The party invitations had dried up, and I was never invited to any group activities either. Not that I cared. I was really over them.

So Rion and I formed a cosy little group of two at lunchtime, except when he was cleaning the lab or helping out in the library, which was every second day. And then I ate alone. Oh joy.

I guess I could've asked to join my old group again, but things weren't the same with Harry anymore. He seemed to think, like the whole school did, that Rion and I were a couple, which we absolutely weren't. We were just friends, although sometimes even that was a stretch. We still argued, and we both managed to say the wrong thing to each other several times a day. But since that disastrous day when I'd kissed him in front of everyone, we'd kind of accepted each other. Sometimes we even liked each other. Just as well, because after that epic kiss, it seemed we were stuck with each other.

So when Mum and Dad kindly said I could have a party if I wanted to as long as there was adult supervision, no alcohol and everyone went home by twelve (what kind of party is *that*?), I turned them down. I didn't have anyone to invite. So now they and Rion were trying to come up with alternate suggestions for my 'big' day.

'What would *you* like to do on your birthday, then?' Rion asked now.

I felt like saying 'get a new life', but that would only result in a lecture about how I was in the top ten percent of the world's population because I was living in relative prosperity in a Western country with a loving family and the ability to get a good education.

I knew all that. But I was also turning sixteen with no friends except an alien who was connected to me for life and, almost as bad, I had gained a kilo and a half and had a pimple coming out on my chin. This was probably due to the junk food I was eating because of my depression. Rion had a perfect body, flawless skin and, having a very logical mind, no idea what depression was because that was too much feeling for him to understand.

Empathy factor? Zilch.

So instead of coming up with a suggestion, I said, 'Dunno. Maybe something exciting, something I've never done before.'

I only said this because I couldn't think of anything else to say. But Rion took it very seriously and furled his brow in thought. Suddenly his eyes lit up again.

'I've got it, the perfect solution.'

'What?' I looked at him with suspicion. My idea of perfect and Rion's were totally different most of the time.

He gave me his crooked smile. 'I'm not going to tell you yet. I think it'll be a surprise. Humans love surprises, don't they?'

'Not unless they're good ones,' I said. 'Seriously, Rion, I appreciate you trying to come up with an idea, but maybe you should drop it. Honestly, my birthday's no big deal. We can just do whatever.' I was trying hard to be diplomatic. No way did I want a surprise birthday activity that was Rion's idea. His next suggestion could be even worse than the State Library, if that was possible.

'Obviously your birthday *is* a big deal because everyone, including yourself and especially your parents, is putting a lot of thought into it. My people don't celebrate birthdays, but I can see that they're significant events here. But don't worry, Zoe. I've come up with a wonderful idea that I'm sure you'll love. I have to discuss it with your parents first, so I won't spoil it by telling you yet.' Rion was getting very excited, for him.

'No, no, it's okay, honestly. Maybe we can have a family barbecue or go out to lunch or something.' I was getting desperate. My parents' idea of fun was even worse than Rion's. And that was saying something.

But Rion had stood up. 'Don't you have some maths homework to do? Better get started on it because after eight pm the brain definitely doesn't work at its best. And you know maths is your worst subject.' That was Rion's 'diplomatic' way of getting rid of me.

I tried once more to deflect him from whatever crazy plan he was going to run past my parents. 'I really don't need anything special organised for my birthday. I'm cool with a lunch out or something, really. Maybe we could even go to the beach.'

It still wasn't very warm and I hated swimming in cold water, but at the moment that idea was looking pretty good—as long as another alien didn't fall on me from out of the sky.

Rion pulled me up from the chair and propelled me towards the door. 'Sure, Zoe, whatever you say. We still have plenty of time to think about it. And now I need to get ready for my shower.' He pushed me out the door and closed it behind me.

Five minutes later I heard him go downstairs instead of to the bathroom. I knew he was going to talk to my parents. When had he learned to be so sneaky? I was filled with a sense of gloomy inevitability. This birthday was going to suck, no matter what we did. I might as well get used to it.

School wasn't totally lame some days, despite, or maybe because of, my lack of friends. I was getting better marks and sometimes I even enjoyed doing assignments, probably because a) Rion nagged me so much that I was studying more, and b) I didn't have a life so I had nothing better to do. Since I was in the last semester of year eleven and next year would be my final year at high school, this was probably a good thing. I still had no idea about what I wanted to do, but if my marks didn't totally suck I might have some choices.

I was reading *Pride and Prejudice* for English downstairs in the study one day when I heard the conversation—the one I'd been dreading. (I would've just watched the movie, but Rion had persuaded me the book was even better. Funnily enough, I didn't actually mind it.) Mum was in the lounge room reading. It was her turn to cook dinner and the smell of vegetables simmering was already wafting through the house.

I heard Dad come in the front door and go into the lounge. 'Where are the kids?' he asked Mum.

The kids. A few days off sixteen and he still called me a kid. And as for Rion, at over four thousand human years of age he had long passed the stage of being a kid, if he ever was one.

'Upstairs, I think,' Mum answered.

I was just about to let them know I was there, and remind them of my mature status, when Dad said, 'Good. I want to talk to you about something.'

I closed my mouth and listened. Maybe I'd finally learn what crazy plan they and Rion had come up with for my birthday. He still wouldn't tell me.

I heard Dad sit down on the sofa; its ancient springs creaking. 'I've been trying to find out something about Rion's parents and his uncle.'

I put down my book and sat up in the chair.

Mum sighed. 'I've tried to question him, gently, of course. I do think he's been through a traumatic experience. He shows all the signs. He tries to change the subject and gets very uncomfortable. And you know how honest he usually is. I haven't managed to find out anything yet other than what he told us on the first day.'

'I've made some enquiries, but no one seems to know anything about this uncle of his,' Dad said. 'I hate to say it, Meg, but I really think we need to contact children's services soon. This situation can't go on.'

'Not yet.' My mum's voice sounded pleading. 'He's settled in so well with us and he's such a good influence on Zoe. She's dropped those unsuitable friends of hers and she's getting better marks. Rion's like part of the family now. Look at how much thought he put into planning Zoe's birthday and how helpful he is around the house.'

'I know,' Dad said. 'I like him too, Meg. And personally I wouldn't mind how long he stayed. But that's not the point, is it? He's a minor and we have a duty to find out the situation with his real family. He's been here for weeks now and we still haven't heard from that "uncle" of his. I'm beginning to think he doesn't exist. I think we have to face the fact that he might've run away from home.' Dad's voice sounded heavy.

All I could feel was a sense of panic. I'd known we'd have to face this sooner or later. But I was hoping for later, much later. Rion never even talked about it, which was unusual for him. He usually planned everything in detail and had at least three back-up contingency plans. But I had no idea how he was going to explain his lengthy stay here when my parents asked him the awkward questions.

I had to talk to him, fast. But I couldn't let my parents know that I'd overheard them.

'I know you're right,' Mum said, 'but let's at least wait until after Zoe's birthday before we do anything. And then we will have to talk to him.'

'Okay,' Dad said, 'I guess it can wait till then. Is that something I smell burning?'

'The veggies!' Mum said. I heard her rush into the kitchen.

'I'll just have a quick shower,' Dad said.

As his footsteps sounded on the stairs, I closed my book and got up. I waited a few minutes until I was sure Dad was in the ensuite and moved to the open study door. Peering out, I checked that Mum was still in the kitchen and then crept up the stairs. I needed to talk to Rion pronto.

Of course he was studying when I entered his room. He looked up and tossed back the fringe that always seemed to get in his way. He'd talked about cutting it, but I persuaded him that it looked cool and for some reason he'd listened to me for once.

'Anything the matter, Zoe?' he asked.

'Plenty.' I plonked down on his bed and told him about Mum and Dad's conversation. 'What are we going to do? We've only got about a week to sort this out.' I couldn't help the note of panic that was in my voice.

He sat back in his chair and thought for a moment.

'Surely you have a plan,' I said, getting impatient. Sometimes Rion just didn't get urgency.

'I knew, of course, that this was inevitable. I just thought it wouldn't happen quite so soon. I thought I had a year or two at least to work it out. I still get so confused by human notions of time.'

'A year or two,' my voice squeaked. 'Five or six weeks is actually a long time to spend with someone with virtually no explanation at all, or at least not a very convincing one. I'm surprised my parents waited this long. And that's only because they like you so much.'

He sighed. 'A month is like a nanosecond in my time, even less. I may have to resort to telling them the truth.'

'The truth?' I said. 'Are you *crazy*? Guess what? If you tell them the truth they'll think you *are* crazy and you'll end up in some mental institution getting all sorts of tests. They'll think you said all this stuff because you were abused or something.'

'A mental institution, that might be interesting. I've never been to one before. It could provide me with many valuable insights into the human condition.'

Sometimes I could've shaken Rion. 'And what about me?' I said. 'What'll happen to me when you're way more than a hundred metres away? Unless they decide to test me, too, and then my life will be totally over. Too bad about any plans I had to do anything with it.'

'Yes, I do see that it could cause problems. Let me rethink,' he said, and closed his eyes.

'Haven't you even thought of this before?' Now I was worried *and* frustrated.

He opened his eyes again. 'Certainly. I'd thought that in a couple of years, which as I said was the timeframe I was working on, when you were eighteen we could get married. That would solve the problem of being apart and also be a socially acceptable conclusion. I could say that my uncle had died in a foreign country and left me some money.

I'm reasonably sure I could get employment of some kind, perhaps at a university where you could also study.'

'Married? Are you *serious*? I don't want to marry you, Rion.' I looked at him in horror.

'Oh, don't go over the top,' he said.

Sometimes Rion used figures of speech that didn't always gel with the situation. But in this case, it was spot on. I was more than "over the top"—I felt like I was about to explode.

'It would only be a marriage on paper,' he said. 'It would just mean that we could be together until my people worked something out. I wouldn't expect anything from you. It would be just like we are now, really.'

'Oh. My. God. I don't believe you.' I tried to calm myself for a moment. This situation was too serious for us to have a fight. Sometimes Rion was clueless, despite the fact that he was so book smart. I tried again.

'Listen, Rion, just forget the whole marriage thing. Even at eighteen I'd be way too young. Mum and Dad would freak out.' Not to mention me. Marriage to an alien, even a good-looking one, was so not on my bucket list, but I was learning to be diplomatic. Rion could be touchy about the weirdest things. 'Besides which, you were never going to last that long here. We need to come up with a plan, like yesterday. Think of it like this. The

Fonz has lost his Thursday comb, his motorbike has broken down and he has a date in ten, no five minutes. Get the urgency?' I was frantically trying to come up with a scenario he would understand from *Happy Days*, his favourite TV program.

'Well, the Fonz still has a comb for every other day of the week, and while he would be upset about his bike it wouldn't really affect his date. With his popularity, she would probably come and pick him up.'

I shook my head. 'What do you see in that show?'

He shrugged. 'It tells me about the interactions of teenagers, which is very helpful at the moment.'

'Yeah, like about sixty years ago.' I searched my brain again for a better analogy. 'Okay, Captain Janeway is on the Borg cube and the teleporter on *Voyager* is broken down. The Borg queen is onto her and she has to get away fast or risk assimilation.'

'That bad, eh?' He thought for a moment. 'You're right, we do need a plan, but try not to worry, Zoe. I'll come up with something, just leave it with me.'

Somehow those words didn't fill me with confidence. I left him thinking and looking out the window.

I went back to my room and flopped on the bed. For the first time in a long while I found myself so wishing that I hadn't gone running on that beach in July.

Chapter Twenty-one

Worrying about my birthday surprise had now taken a very distant second place to worrying about the Rion problem. He wouldn't talk about it with me except to say he was 'working on it'. I was beginning to think he still didn't get the urgency at all, so I came up with some ideas of my own. Or at least I tried to.

Maybe we could say his uncle had come back and then we could persuade someone to impersonate him. But who? No one sprang to mind.

Maybe we could say that the uncle had died and Rion's mum said he could live with us. Again, there was no one to play the parts for us.

I was getting desperate.

Finally it was Saturday, the day before my birthday, and Mum and Dad were acting very mysterious and a little excited. Jeez, I hoped they weren't planning something really dumb like a surprise birthday party. I couldn't see any sign of preparations, but Mum was sneaky about stuff like that. Probably came from being a primary school teacher and planning stuff for all those unsuspecting little kids she taught.

Rion always seemed to have his head in a book and would hardly talk to me. I so wished my best friend hadn't moved away, or at least that Harry was talking to me normally again.

That night everyone wanted to go to bed early. Very strange.

'Oh, look at the time, I think I'll go to bed,' Mum said, giving a fake yawn.

We were all watching *Star Trek Voyager* on Netflix. Dad and Rion (of course) loved science fiction, and usually so did I, but tonight I was too on edge, worrying not just about tomorrow but about what would happen to Rion. I glanced down at my phone. It was 9:45 pm. Oh yes, definitely time for bed—if you were eight years old.

'Yes, I think I'll turn in too,' Dad said, 'I've had a very big week.' This was from a man who regularly went to bed at midnight.

Rion added his bit. 'I'm also feeling tired. Must be all that studying I did this week.' As if he didn't do that every day.

'You may as well get an early night too, Zoe,' Mum said, flicking off the television.

'Okay, what's up, you guys?' I looked at them with suspicion.

'Nothing,' Mum said, sounding totally unconvincing. She had not missed her calling as an actor.

'This has to do with my birthday, doesn't it?'

If I had to go to bed early it must mean I had to get up early. Nothing that sounded even remotely appealing went with that. What had they done, sign me up for a gym membership or something? Maybe a personal trainer was coming around first thing in the morning. Did I look that out of shape? Rion was always saying I wasn't fit.

'I hope this has nothing to do with early-morning exercise.' I said. Then another thought occurred to me. 'You haven't bought me a bike or anything like that, have you? We aren't going on some family ride in the park, are we? You do realise I'll be sixteen tomorrow, don't you, and not ten?'

'Just go to bed, Zoe. You'll find out in the morning,' Dad said.

Mum had already gone upstairs and Rion was grinning at me stupidly. I decided I hated birthdays, especially ones that had surprises. But no one would tell me anything, so I went to bed and pretended to go to sleep. I was so not looking forward to tomorrow.

I was totally convinced that my family had gone nuts when my mum woke me up. It was completely dark outside.

'Happy birthday, darling,' she said.

I opened a sleepy eye. 'What?'

She gave me another gentle shake. 'Come on, time to get up and celebrate your special day.'

'But it's dark outside. What time is it?' I looked at the illuminated clock next to my bed. 'Mum, it's three forty-five in the morning!'

'I know, honey, but we have something really special planned for you and you need to get up now.' She pulled the blankets off me, proving she wasn't the nice, sweet person she pretended to be. 'Rise and shine,' she added in a fake happy voice.

'Can't it wait, like, four or five hours?' I tried to pull the blankets back over me but failed because Mum had a good grip on them.

'We'll pick up coffee and hot chocolate on the way. Now get up and put on something warm. It's a little chilly.' She was clearly going to wait until I got out of bed. I'd never realised my mother liked to torture people. Hidden depths, much.

I struggled to a sitting position.

She held out a pair of jeans to me. 'I'm giving you five minutes, tops, and then I'll be back if you're not downstairs.' She blew me a kiss and left.

I'm not a morning person. Yes, I can function after seven am on a school morning in that I get up, grab cereal and coffee, and get myself to the school bus. But being awake in the morning is not my natural state. I hate getting up early. This, however, was not early. This was the middle of the night. I was too tired to even imagine the horrible plans they had for me. Best to get it over with.

I pulled on my jeans and then realised I'd put them over my PJs. It was going to be a long day.

When I went into the kitchen they were all there, grinning at me.

Dad gave me a hug. 'Happy birthday, sweetheart,' he said.

'What's happening?' I stifled a yawn and looked at them all with suspicion.

'It's your birthday surprise,' Rion said, and also gave me an awkward hug.

He still had a lot to learn about human contact, though I had to admit he'd mastered kissing. Where,

I wondered, did *that* thought come from? I decided it must be because my brain was sleep deprived.

'You're going to love this,' Mum said, looking at her watch. 'Come on, we'd better leave if we're going to be on time.'

'Where are we going?' I was still completely puzzled as to what was happening.

'Nerang.' Dad headed out the door, jingling the keys.

I shook my head in disbelief. 'What on earth is in Nerang?' I knew it was on the south side of Brisbane, but other than that I had no clue about what was there.

'You'll see,' Mum said, following Dad out the door.

I nudged Rion. 'What's going on? Come on, spill.'

'I never spill anything if I can help it, Zoe.' He winked at me. So funny, not.

The long drive didn't improve things, apart from the hot chocolate. After that, since no one would tell me anything, I closed my eyes and tried to sleep. But even though I wasn't delighted at being woken up in the middle of the night, I had to admit I was curious about what they had planned. I wracked my brain to think about what it could be but came up blank.

We pulled into the carpark of an almost deserted shopping centre in Nerang. There were one or two cars parked there and a minibus. I tumbled out of the car and looked at the bus with its colourful writing splashed on the side. And then it clicked. I looked at my parents and Rion, and they smiled back at me.

'We're going on a hot-air balloon ride!'

'It was Rion's idea, and I thought it was a wonderful way to spend your sixteenth birthday,' Mum said.

'I was impressed myself,' Dad said, nodding. 'He even put some money towards it, though he didn't really need to.'

I gave Rion a proper hug this time and he hugged me back. 'Thank you so much.'

'You like the idea, then?' he asked.

'Like it? I *love* it. This is so much better than a gym membership or a personal trainer,' I said, and laughed.

'Huh?' He looked puzzled.

'Never mind.' I looked at the bus with its Brisbane Hot Air Ballooning sign. 'So, where's the balloon?'

'Come on,' Dad said. 'They're going to drive us to the site.'

Suddenly all my sleepiness disappeared. Besides our family, there were two other couples, one from Japan, and another celebrating their anniversary or something. Everyone was super-excited, even the old couple who had done it before.

'You'll love it,' the woman said. 'Gus and I have been up a couple times, once overseas and once on the

Gold Coast. We're addicted now.' She laughed and her husband gave her hand a squeeze.

Dawn was just breaking when we got to the field. The balloon was already unpacked. We watched as they inflated it and a huge orange ball grew before our eyes.

I was a little nervous as we got into the large basket. Not that I would ever have admitted it to anyone, but I was scared of heights. But although I was scared, I was also kind of excited. I stood next to Rion, with Mum and Dad just behind us. My hands gripped the side of the basket as they let go the ropes and the first blast of hot air started to lift us. My stomach gave a lurch. Then I felt Rion cover one of my hands with his.

'There's nothing to be scared of, Zoe,' he said. 'I researched the safety aspects and there's very little danger in hot-air ballooning. And this particular company has one of the highest safety records.'

I looked down at the ground, which was slowly getting further away. This isn't so bad, I thought, and my nerves started to settle. As we rose into the air the landscape spread below us; the trees, distant houses and cars becoming smaller and smaller, like toys.

'Wow,' I said.

'Look over there, at the sun,' Mum said, pointing to the east.

Over the horizon, the sun was all golden and fiery as it lit the sky.

'Way cool,' I said.

A slight breeze blew us upward, and even though my stomach did a flip-flop it was kind of fun. Our pilot started to point out landmarks as we drifted across the sky. I almost felt I could touch the wispy clouds above.

Then I looked over at Rion. His face was white and drawn, and his eyes were closed. Was he sick or something? Maybe he had a fear of heights, too. 'Hey, are you okay?' He didn't answer me. He was missing all this and he was the one who had planned it all. His hand had gone cold. I squeezed it and said, 'Rion, what's up?'

Again there was no answer. I was about to tell Mum and Dad that Rion didn't look well when he opened his eyes again. He blinked and then shook his head.

'Rion, what's wrong?' I said.

He looked down at me for a moment as if he didn't even know me. His hand dropped from mine. 'I'm fine,' he said, then turned away and stared up at the sky.

The rest of the trip was totally awesome except for the fact that I was worried about Rion. He seemed to snap back to normal after a few minutes, but he was very quiet for the rest of the trip.

We landed near a winery in the hills of the hinterland where we were going to have a champagne breakfast. Well, champagne for Mum and Dad, orange juice for Rion and me. Typical, my birthday and they get to drink. Never mind. Everything else was great. The restaurant, which had been told about my special day, even gave me a cupcake with a sparkler on it and everyone sang 'Happy Birthday'. Kind of lame, but cute.

After the shuttle bus had taken us back to the carpark and we were heading for the car, Dad asked, 'Well, what did you think of your birthday surprise, Zoe?'

'Best birthday ever,' I said. 'Thanks so much, Mum and Dad and Rion.'

I gave them all hugs again and we piled into the car. Rion was still quiet, and it was really starting to worry me. Had he had some kind of episode up there, like epilepsy or something? Maybe his alien self was starting to reject his physical body. But there was no chance to talk to him with Mum and Dad in the car. I'd have to wait until we got home.

It was nearly noon when we pulled into the driveway. Mum went for a nap, Dad disappeared behind a newspaper, and I headed upstairs. I was no sooner in my bedroom than there was a knock on the door.

Rion came in. 'We need to talk,' he said.

'Yeah, I was going to ask you what happened up there in the balloon.'

'It's happened,' he said, crossing his arms and leaning against the door. There was a look on his face that I couldn't understand.

'What's happened?'

'My people, they've contacted me.'

Chapter Twenty-two

I collapsed onto my bed. 'What? When? How?' I said, going through every question word I could think of.

'When we were in the balloon,' he said, 'do you remember how close we were to some of the clouds? Well, one of them had a colony of my people in it. They've finally realised what happened to me, after I've been trying to contact them for weeks, although I can't complain that it took them so long because in terms of our concept of time it's been a nanosecond.'

'So that was why you went so pale and everything. I wondered what was happening to you.'

'Yes, I believe so. In your terms, you could say I had an out-of-body experience. Very strange.'

'But you've never had a body before now. You were just a bubble of consciousness,' I said, 'so it couldn't have been all that strange. You were just going back to what you used to be.'

'No, that's not actually true. On my home planet, which is in the Orion constellation, we do have physical bodies. But when we volunteer for the space exploration program we sacrifice our physical state and become pure consciousness so we can travel more efficiently to other parts of the universe.'

I sat up. 'Really? You've never told me much about your life.' Images of science-fiction shows and movies I'd watched flickered through my mind. I wondered what kind of bodies his people had. Would they be all creepy and lizardy, or would they be all big eyed and ET like?

He shrugged. 'You've never been that interested, Zoe, and, besides, we've had a lot to deal with.'

I realised that what he said was true. I had been too self-absorbed in many ways. I should've been more curious, more empathetic toward Rion instead of always finding fault with him. I felt kind of ashamed that I hadn't given him more thought.

'I've been selfish,' I said, trying to be honest. 'I should've been more interested in who you are and where you came from. Instead all I've thought about is my own problems.'

'That's okay, Zoe. Being self-centred is a human trait, I believe.'

'Not with everyone.' I thought of my mum, who always thought of others, and Harry, who had been kind and always there for me until recently.

I looked at Rion again. 'So what happened to your body? Did they store it someplace for when you go back?' Even saying it seemed kind of surreal.

He shook his head. 'No, after one's consciousness is extracted, the body dies a natural death. I can never go back.'

I think my jaw might have dropped. 'What? Never? That's awful. It's like dying.'

'Not at all,' Rion said in a very matter-of-fact way. 'We actually live much longer that way, longer than if we had physical bodies. To be a space traveller on my planet is considered a great honour. We're searching out the secrets of the universe and exploring new forms of beings. It's a noble cause.'

'Like on *Star Trek*,' I said.

'Somewhat,' he said, 'but without an organic existence, of course. I've often wondered if Gene Roddenberry was host to one of our people. Some of his ideas were so advanced.'

'But you said you were studying us to take us over. I don't think that's a very noble cause, or very advanced, at least not from a human point of view.'

Rion smiled his crooked grin. 'I only said that to freak you out. It was a joke. You were so determined to think the worst of me.'

'Jeez, some joke.' These aliens clearly had a different sense of humour to ours. 'So,' I said, feeling curious, although I wasn't sure I would totally like the answer, 'what did you look like before you were a soap bubble?'

'I resembled the body I'm in now.'

I looked at his strong arms, which were crossed against his broad chest. His dark hair hung just over his eyes, though I could still see them, dark and kind of intense. He didn't look like any alien I'd ever imagined. 'Seriously? You look human.'

He gave a small laugh. 'Or perhaps, more correctly, humans look like us. We have a similar atmosphere to Earth's, but we've been around much longer and have evolved into a highly intelligent, sentient species that's still trying to become an ideal society. We've progressed more than you have on Earth, but we're still on a "learning curve", as you might say.'

'Oh. I thought you'd chosen that body so you'd look like us,' I said.

'Actually, no, it was easier to materialise as the self I was. And it's been … nice to be like my physical self again.'

'So how old were you when you went space travelling?'

'About the same age as you,' he said. 'We volunteer when we're young so we don't have too many ties to our organic, physical forms. Once we become pure consciousness, age is irrelevant. And the plus side is that we live virtually forever, which wouldn't happen on my home planet. So there are compensations in giving up our bodies.'

Wow, I thought, but was careful not to say it out loud. So Rion looked exactly like ... Rion. It made him seem more real than ever. I wondered what would happen now that his people had contacted him. 'So what did they say? Your people, that is.'

He hesitated a moment.

'C'mon, Rion, are you going to change back into what you were? Are you going back to the mothership or what?' Even as I asked him, I felt everything inside me twist. I didn't want Rion as a consciousness inside me again, but I didn't want to lose contact with him either. I was beginning to realise how much I'd miss him.

'Mother*cloud*,' he said with a sigh. 'I don't suppose you'll ever get it right.' He looked sad. 'My superior, though understandably disapproving of my materialising into a physical body, was surprisingly magnanimous. He gave me a choice. You'll be relieved to know, however, that no matter what I choose the bond between us will be severed.'

'Oh,' I said. I had mixed feelings about that. Yeah, it would be good to have my life back, but I was getting kind of used to having an alien around. 'What were the choices?'

He shifted position, moving to the chair in the corner where my old Pooh Bear sat. He picked it up and put it on his lap. It was kind of funny but cute to see him with my old teddy bear. I wondered if this would be one of the last times I'd see Rion in this hunky human body, which I now realised was his real one.

'I could dematerialise and go back to one of the motherclouds. It would mean finding a new host. The bond between you and me would be severed and you would be free. Isn't that what you want, Zoe?' His eyes met mine.

My heart did a little flip-flop. Did I? 'Does that mean we wouldn't talk, like, ever again?'

He nodded. 'Of course,' he said, 'that would be inappropriate. Once I'm with my new host my communications will be solely with that human. It's highly unlikely we'd have anything to do with each other ever again.'

Six weeks ago that statement would've had me doing cartwheels. Now I felt sick. 'I would really miss you, Rion.'

Obviously the feeling wasn't mutual because all he said was, 'You'd get used to it, and it would solve the problem with your parents. You made me realise the other day that I can't stay here much longer. I definitely can't use the timeframe I was thinking of.'

Had I? Me and my big mouth. Not having Rion there to give me lectures about healthy living, food, study and information on just about every topic ever invented; not having someone to go to school with, to have lunch with, to talk about my problems with; not knowing that he was there and if he got too far away from me I could physically feel his absence. Most of the time that distance thing was annoying, but sometimes it was … comforting. It was like feeling someone was there for you 24/7.

'What was the other choice?'

He stood up again, put down the bear and looked out the window.

Just then I heard my mum's voice. 'Zoe, honey, Gran's on the phone,' she called. 'She wants to wish you happy birthday.'

'Coming,' I called back. I'd have to go downstairs to the landline. My gran didn't like calling people on mobile phones. She was convinced they gave you cancer.

I got up and turned to Rion. 'Well? What was the other choice?'

'You'd better go talk to your grandmother. I'll speak to you later,' he said, then went out of my room and into his own, and closed the door.

Damn, talk about timing. I went downstairs.

I love my gran. She gets me and is always in my corner. But today, even though it was my birthday, I wished she'd waited until later on to call. I tried not to show my impatience and put on my cheerful voice. 'Hi, Gran.'

'Happy birthday, darling,' she said. 'I wish I could be there to celebrate it with you, but I hear you've had a wonderful experience up in a hot-air balloon.'

'Yeah, it was awesome.'

'That's on my bucket list, that and skydiving. Perhaps you and I will do that next year.' Even though she didn't use mobile phones, Gran was totally cool. 'Anyway, dear, how's that young man of yours?'

I was puzzled. 'What young man?'

'The one staying with you, of course. I've been hearing good things about him from your mum. He seems like a lovely boy.'

'Yeah, he's okay. But Gran, he's just a friend, nothing else.' I wanted to set the record straight on that, particularly since he probably wouldn't be around that much longer.

'He seems like a very good friend to me, planning your birthday surprise and going to all that trouble. Didn't you two go on a date?'

My mum had a lot to answer for sometimes. Did she have to tell Gran *everything*?

'We only went bowling, Gran. It was just a fun night, nothing special.'

'Those dates are the best kind, believe me,' she said. 'When you find someone you can have fun with, who's thoughtful and kind, that, my dear, is what we call a keeper.'

I kept down a big sigh, which felt suspiciously like a teeny-tiny sob. None of that, I told myself firmly. Get a grip.

Gran was as intuitive as ever. 'But never mind about that,' she said, 'tell me more about that hot-air balloon ride. They don't have age restrictions, do they?'

I talked to Gran for a few more minutes and then said goodbye after promising to visit her in Sydney soon. That would have caused problems before today because I couldn't go that far away unless I took Rion, but now it wouldn't be an issue.

Thinking of Rion, I went back upstairs to continue our conversation. What was his other choice? I was so curious I couldn't get up the stairs fast enough. He wasn't in his room. I went downstairs to look for him.

'Where's Rion?' I asked Dad.

He looked up from his paper. 'He's gone for a walk, I think,' he said, then disappeared into the pages of *The Australian* again.

I went out the front door and looked up and down the street, not seeing him anywhere. I knew he couldn't go too far from me. We'd both been careful about that after the couple of times when we forgot. The feeling of sickness, nausea and everything was not good. Right now I didn't feel too bad, so either he wasn't far away or the link between us was already severed. I really had mixed feelings about that.

Maybe he was at the park at the end of the street. That wasn't too far away. I started to walk in that direction and then began to notice the beginnings of the sick sensation. Nope, link not severed. I was starting to realise how lonely I would be if that happened. I'd never felt so connected to anyone before, and I'd miss that.

I went back to the house and gazed around the garden, my eyes hitting on the shed. I thought back to the first night he came home with me and I'd put him in Dad's boat. That seemed ages ago now. So much had happened since then.

The door to the shed was unlocked, so that was a positive sign. Even though it was daytime, the small, dirty shed window didn't let in much light. I could see the boat, but I couldn't make out if anyone was in it or not. I went over and climbed up on the deck.

'Rion?'

There was no answer and I couldn't see him. False alarm. Then I peered inside the cabin. There, curled up on one of the bunks, was Rion. His eyes were closed, but somehow I didn't think he was asleep.

'Rion, what's up?'

He opened his eyes and looked at me but didn't say anything.

I went down the cabin steps and sat next to him. 'Tell me, what's the matter?'

Rion always seemed to be the one solving my problems and never the other way around. It struck me again that sometimes I hadn't been the best of friends to him. I had never, not once, considered how awful it must have been for him to be separated from his people, not knowing how he would get back to them. And he had never given me a guilt trip for the fact that he couldn't dematerialise into that soap bubble he'd been, that 'pure consciousness', as he called it.

He sighed and looked away. 'Don't worry, Zoe, I'm fine, I'm just thinking a few things out.'

'You want to share?' I drew up my legs and settled down at the foot of the bunk.

'I'm still making my mind up about something.' He closed his eyes again. 'You might as well go inside and have one of those unhealthy snacks you love so much. After all, it is your birthday.'

'I don't care about that. I'm kind of worried about you. A first, I know,' I said and smiled.

'Seriously, Zoe,' he said, sounding for once like the teen he wasn't, 'I don't think you can do much. This is something I have to decide myself.'

'Maybe, but sometimes it does help to talk to someone else. Please tell me, Rion. You know we're still connected, and somehow it feels more than a physical thing right now. I can't settle, or do anything, really, until I know you're all right.'

Giving another sigh, he uncurled himself, and sat up beside me. 'I can see you're not going to go away until I do.'

'So true,' I said. 'You know how determined I can be.'

'Actually, I think stubborn is a better word.' He smiled his crooked smile at me.

'Always the diplomat, not,' I said, and gave him a light punch on the arm. 'C'mon, my alien, tell me what the trouble is.'

'What did you just call me?'

'My alien,' I said. 'That's what I sometimes call you in my head now that you're no longer a soap bubble. It's one of the politer terms I use.'

'Not just *the* alien, but *my* alien?'

'Yeah, well, that's the way it seems, seeing as we're sort of close and all.'

He put his head on one side and looked at me. 'That's nice. I like it.'

My stomach did that flip-floppy thing again.

We sat quietly for a few minutes and then Rion spoke. 'Okay, I guess I should tell you what else my supervisor told me. He said that my other choice, besides returning to the mothercloud and finding a new host, was to remain in my human form.'

'You mean like you are now?' I was puzzled about why he seemed so upset. 'That's good, isn't it?' *I* thought it was good, anyway. I wasn't ready to lose Rion yet.

'Yes and no,' he said. 'First of all, you and I would have no connection. We wouldn't have to worry about the distance between us making us sick anymore, and you'd be free to live a normal life.'

So far I wasn't seeing the downside to this.

He continued. 'But the difference would be that I would become completely normal—completely human, that is. I would live the lifespan of a natural human being, growing old and eventually dying. And if I decided to stay in this organic existence, there'd be no turning back. Also, it was felt that I would gain much greater knowledge about humans by having the real-life experience of being human myself, rather than just observing them. It's an experiment my people have never tried before, to become one of you.'

I was feeling excited now. 'So you could be normal? We could still be friends and everything?'

He nodded.

'That's great,' I said. 'And then when you finish your human life you could go back to your mothercloud, share all your knowledge and then start over again.'

This time he shook his head. 'No, didn't you understand what I said about no turning back? As a human, when I died that would be it. I would be *completely* human. I would never go back to my people again. In fact, I might even forget who or what I'd been. My memories would be taken from me so my people could learn from them, but I might have no knowledge of that. I don't know all the details yet, but if I choose to be human that would be the end. I wouldn't be part of my race any more.'

'Oh, I see.'

I thought about it. Rion would lose everything he had, everything he was, if he became human. I remembered the fairytale *The Little Mermaid*, where the mermaid gives up her voice so she can have legs and be with the prince. In a way that's what Rion would be doing. He'd have to give up so much. Only he could decide if it was worth the price he'd have to pay. The thought of him leaving, and me never seeing him again, was unbearable. But that was beside the point. This was about Rion, not me.

'That's a big deal, huh?' I said, realising how inadequate the words sounded.

'Yes, Zoe, a very big deal.'

I squeezed his hand.

Chapter Twenty-three

'So, what have you decided?' I asked. I knew the answer I wanted to hear, even though it was selfish of me.

'I don't know yet,' he said. 'That's what I'm thinking about. If you'd asked me that when I first materialised I wouldn't have had to even consider it. I would've gone back to my pure form and returned to my people until I had another host. That's the existence I've lived for thousands of years, and it's the mission I've dedicated my life to. The thrill of learning about your world through the eyes of so many diverse human creatures, and then sharing that knowledge with my world so we could understand yours even better, is something that gave my existence meaning and purpose. I'd never regretted giving up my organic physical existence before. But after that night of the party, when I materialised, I realised what I'd been missing. After a while I became used to being human and everything changed.'

'How?'

'Let me explain.' He picked up my hand, running his thumb along my fingers. 'To feel the warmth and softness of touch is something I'd forgotten. To inhale the scent of flowers in your garden, or the perfume you sometimes wear is intoxicating. Even to taste the food I've given you all those lectures about is amazing. I still remember that first French fry you gave me. It was like opening a window on a whole new world of sensations. In all the years I've inhabited hosts, I've never felt anything like it. It's true that I materialised once before, but I didn't stay in that form long enough to become addicted to being human. And now I don't know if I can give all that up.'

He still had my hand and I gave it another squeeze. I didn't want to say this, but I knew I had to. For once I had to stop thinking about myself.

'But if you stay human you'll lose your people. And instead of living for another couple of thousand years, you might only have another sixty or seventy. You'll have to give up the mission you've dedicated everything to. Is it worth it?'

'That's the question I've been asking myself all afternoon. But there's something else I'd miss if I went back to my former state.'

'What?'

'You. I would miss being with you, talking to you, even arguing with you. I would miss,' he stopped and gave me a shy smile, 'I would miss never being able to kiss you again.'

Okay, I've never actually been hit with a bowling ball in my chest, but that's what it felt like now. Here was this beautiful boy telling me that he liked kissing me, even though we'd only kissed twice. The feeling was so mutual, and I might not see or hear from him ever again.

'I would miss that, too,' I said.

And then his face bent closer and I felt my breath catch. I moved towards him. His hands encircled my waist and drew me in. Wrapping my arms around his neck, I lifted my face to his. His lips were warm and firm, and his arms tightened, drawing me even closer so I could feel that broad, muscled chest and hear the steady beat of his heart, so near to mine.

For a few seconds, or maybe it was centuries, I don't know, I was lost in the sweetest kiss I had ever known. Then he pulled away and I felt like when you come off the rollercoaster at Dreamworld, dizzy and disoriented but wanting to do it all again.

'You could stay,' I couldn't help saying. 'You could stay with us. Mum and Dad won't mind. We could go to school together, to university. Maybe we could even be together.' I looked at him, hoping. 'It doesn't matter to me that you're an alien. No one has to know.'

Instantly I knew I'd said the wrong thing. His eyes darkened even more, like they always did when he was upset. He probably thought I was ashamed of him. I tried to explain. 'I mean, there's nothing wrong with you being different, like ... not human. It's kind of interesting. I could learn so much from you, seeing as you've lived so long and everything.'

I was only making it worse, waffling on. The expression on Rion's face became even more serious. If I could've taken back those last words, I would have, in an instant. But it was too late.

For a moment neither of us said anything, then his eyes caught mine and I could see the sadness in them. 'But I *am* an "alien",' he said. 'We're from different worlds, Zoe, and nothing can change that.'

'It doesn't matter, not to me.'

'Not now, but it might in the future.'

I opened my mouth to protest, and he gently put a finger on my lips. 'You should be free to live your life and be with someone of your own kind, not someone who has lived for four thousand years in another existence. It isn't just who I am now, but who I've been. I should never have materialised as a human. I don't regret it, but it was a foolish mistake and it's not one I want you to pay for.' He paused for a moment and I knew what he was going to say. 'I'm so sorry,' he said, 'but I have to go back.'

I blinked to keep back the tears. I wanted to protest and argue with him, but I could see the determination in his eyes. I made one last effort to convince him. 'You don't have to be with me. You could stay just for you.'

'In that case I *should* go back.'

He tried to explain. It was his destiny, he told me. He'd sacrificed everything on his home planet—his family, his home and his very physical existence—for this mission to explore and study the universe. He couldn't give that up, not even now. He couldn't disappoint his parents, who had let him go willingly all those years ago, or the others who had competed with him for his place in the space program and missed out. This was bigger than him.

For the first time I realised that my alien was kind of heroic.

I had to be strong. I had to let him go. 'Okay,' I said, 'I understand.' And I did.

We walked back to the house together, hand in hand. That night we had the birthday dinner and the birthday cake with my parents. There were a few more phone calls from aunts, uncles, cousins, and even a friend or two. We tried, Rion and I, to act normal and even happy. But I knew we had said our goodbyes.

I had tried to be strong. But it didn't stop me crying into my pillow that night. Rion knew I was upset, but he didn't know just how upset. My sixteenth birthday was both the best and the worst day of my life.

When I woke up the next morning, I knew he had gone. I felt like there was a big hole in my chest. I knew I had lost something really special that I would never have again.

When I went down to breakfast, Mum and Dad were waiting for me with sad, sympathetic looks.

'Darling, we have something to tell you,' Mum said.

'Rion has left,' Dad said. He was never one to beat around the bush. If something was bad news he thought it was better to tell you right away, like ripping off a plaster quickly. 'His uncle came for him last night.'

Hearing the words affected me more than I'd expected. I blinked away the moisture that was beginning to form in my eyes. I turned away and poured a cup of coffee so they wouldn't see how upset I was.

I remembered that Rion had said his people would come up with a plan to help him leave so no one would ask questions. Maybe the 'uncle' had been another alien who had materialised briefly to provide Rion with an easy exit. By now they were probably both happy little soap bubbles in a cloud, waiting for the next host. I tried not to feel bitter. It had been Rion's choice, and he had given good reasons for making it. I had to respect that.

'His uncle was quite determined to leave with Rion straightaway and didn't want to stay overnight so Rion could say goodbye to you,' Mum said. 'We tried to persuade him that they would both be welcome, but he said he was going to take Rion on one of his trips and they needed to leave immediately. I believe they're going back to Brazil, although I'm not sure. He wasn't a very forthcoming man.'

'Not forthcoming?' Dad said. 'He was damn rude. Rion hasn't heard from him in all this time and suddenly he turns up on our doorstep demanding to see his nephew and then takes him away in the dead of night—'

'He did thank us for looking after Rion,' Mum said.

'Barely,' Dad said. 'Wouldn't even stay for a cup of tea.'

I took my cup and turned to face them again, sinking down on a kitchen chair. 'How was Rion?' I tried to keep my voice neutral.

'He was perfectly polite, as usual,' Mum said, sniffling. 'He thanked us for having him and told us he would miss us. He said to tell you goodbye. Then, like the well-behaved young man he is, he went off with his uncle.'

'Who didn't leave a forwarding address or anything. I don't know if we should've let Rion go so easily without some proof that the man actually was his uncle,' Dad said, pushing his toast to one side and folding his arms.

'Well, Rion said he was, and he wouldn't go off so willingly with a stranger, would he?' Mum said logically. 'He's not a stupid boy.' She grabbed a tissue from the box on the table and blew her nose. 'I'm sure he'll be in touch, though.'

I knew he wouldn't. 'I don't really feel like breakfast. I think I'll catch the early bus to school.' I escaped before they could see the tears gathering in my eyes again. This time I wouldn't be able to stop them from falling.

Life sucked. Everyone at school missed Rion at first, but after a while it was as if he hadn't even been there. It was just me who couldn't forget. I felt like everything in life had turned kind of grey.

I never went back to Jas's group. She was still pretty horrible to me, though she no longer saw me as any kind of competition. Harry's group let me back in, and Harry gradually started to act normally with me. Then, in term four, he got glandular fever and had to stay at home for the last month of the school year so I didn't even have him to talk to.

I became a loner. Parties and gatherings had lost their appeal. About the only thing I did was go to school and back. On the plus side I studied more, because now that I'd gotten into the habit it wasn't so bad. I also watched *Happy Days*, because it reminded me of Rion.

When it was cloudy, I would look up and wonder if he had found a new host yet, or if he was still up there, waiting. Did he ever think of me? On clear nights I would look out my bedroom window to see if I could find the Orion constellation. Then I became lost in imagining what his planet was like.

Mostly, I didn't cry any more. Only when I went to bed, and sometimes when I'd had a bad day and wanted to talk to him about it.

I finished year eleven and did pretty well. Mum and Dad were pleased with me. I knew they put it down to Rion's influence. They missed him, too, though they didn't talk about him much. Maybe they realised how badly I felt and didn't want to make it worse. They suggested I go and visit my gran in Sydney for part of the Christmas holidays. I knew they were worried about me.

Then one day I went into the shed to look at our boat. Dad would be giving it a clean and a check soon so we could use it in the holidays. I wanted to have one last look at it first and remember that kiss Rion and I had shared on my sixteenth birthday.

I climbed into the boat and sat on the bunk. On the floor in the corner, an empty red liquorice bag and a cardboard hot-chip cup caught my eye. Next to them was a crinkled receipt. I bent down to pick it up. Red liquorice strips and hot chips were two of my favourite treats, but I hadn't been here recently so they couldn't be mine. In fact, I hadn't been here since the day we'd last kissed.

I looked again at the receipt, peering at the date. It was only a month old, and Rion had left us over three months ago. Who had been here since then? It wasn't Mum or Dad because they both said they dreaded having to clean the boat, and they hadn't opened the shed in months. Besides, chips and liquorice weren't snacks that either of them would be likely to have. So who was it?

I could think of only one other person who would come here. One other person who knew my eating habits so well and told me he would never forget his first French fry. I felt a smile curve my lips as I thought of the possible answer.

There were a few questions in my mind, but right now all I could think of was one thing— maybe Rion hadn't gone back to the mothercloud after all. Maybe he'd decided to become human, but for some reason hadn't told me yet.

I took the receipt and put it in my jeans pocket. It would go next to the pressed yellow flower he had given me on our first date. Maybe—that was a wonderful word—I would see him again.

I felt a small hope starting to grow, and with it came a determination to discover what had really happened to Rion. Determination or stubbornness, take your pick. Either way, I wasn't ready to let go. Maybe the connection between us hadn't gone completely, because I felt something strongly.

One day I was going to see my alien again.

Acknowledgements

A big thank-you to all those who have given me encouragement, feedback, wine, coffee, and especially chocolate! To Ruth, for making my website a reality, being a beta reader, and in general being on my cheer squad. To Richard, who always gave me encouragement, especially in being entrepreneurial and doing it yourself. A special tip of the hat to Book Cover Cafe, whose professional help and advice made everything so much easier. And huge acknowledgement to the Romance Writers Association of Australia, a fabulous organisation that nurtures, encourages and celebrates all its members, from newbies to award-winning pros. Also, heartfelt gratitude to the many writers and friends whose books have inspired me and shown me that I was not alone on this journey. Finally my husband, Rob, who supplied the love and the chocolate, and always made me feel I could do it.

About the Author

Robin Martin has been a writer and a teacher for many years. Originally from Canada, she has lived and worked in several countries but now lives just outside Brisbane. Writing has always been her passion, and in recent years she has written several novels and short stories for adults and young adults. When she is not plotting stories, she loves reading everything from cereal boxes to long books that she can get lost in. Though she still loves travelling, these days she is content to write about adventures rather than live them, although her current series has tempted her to consider hot air ballooning in the hope that she might contact aliens.

Visit Robin at her website, www.robinmartinthomas.com to sign up for her newsletter and find out more about her next book, *The Alien Within*.

www.robinmartinthomas.com

Printed in Australia
AUOC02n1504150217
283059AU00002B/2/P